Girl On Girl On Girl: 15 Erotic Stories About Lesbians

Curated by Hannah Butler

Features:

Maxx Harper

Hannah Butler

Alexia Engles

Krista Collar

L.J. Harper

Jerry Forrest

Contents

First Time Lesbian Submissive Enjoys Bondage, Gaping, and Watersports

Maxx Harper

"We really do need to talk, pet. I want to make sure that we're on the same page about… things." Elise, my new roommate and first lesbian experience, poured the eggs evenly between two plates, setting one in front of me and one beside it, and grabbing some sliced fruit from the fridge, sat down. I watched her take a few bites, and then she put down her fork and looked at me.

"Maxx, you should know by now that I have very particular tastes when it comes to sex." I blushed, thinking about her tongue in my ass in the shower the night before. "Yes, I think I've made some of them pretty clear. I just want to make sure that you fully understand what it will be like to be with me. I'd like this to be permanent, but I want to make sure that I won't scare you off."

"Elise, really, I can't imagine you doing anything that would make me leave. Haven't I enjoyed everything you've done so far?" I quickly thought through everything. Sure, I had been apprehensive when she started putting her finger in my ass, but I hadn't told her to stop, not even when she added the second. I had taken four fingers into my pussy with pleasure before that. It was obvious that I liked the things she wanted to do to me.

"Pet, you were wonderful. Better than I ever would have expected for someone so new to all of this, but last night was just the tip of the iceberg. I want, I need, to do things to you that will make last night look like a family film in comparison, and I like being in control while I do them. No deep dark secret why, it's just what gets me off. I get so much pleasure from helping you experience new things and showing you just what your fucking hot body is capable of doing, of taking." She was gripping both of my shoulders hard at that point, as if to drive home how serious she was. "If you trust me, I'll make you feel so damn good." Her hands lowered, spreading my robe apart to fondle my breasts. "Do you trust me, pet?"

I held my breath for a moment, and then nodded. She pinched my nipples painfully, kissing me hard. "Fucking fantastic. Finish eating. In five minutes, come to my room," she said, shoveling her remaining eggs into her mouth. She stood up, placed her plate in the sink, and quickly walked off. I glanced at the clock as I finished my breakfast, figuring that she would probably be a stickler on time. Exactly five minutes later I put my plate in the sink as well and walked across the house. She had opened all of the curtains, and the room was full of bright sunlight. All of the bedding had been removed except for the fitted sheet, and there were ropes of some sort coming from each of the four posts. A big black box sat on the side table, a small glass jar beside it. Elise came out from the bathroom, her hair slicked back into a tight bun, a scarf dangling from her hand.

"On the bed, face down," she ordered. I hesitated for just a moment, unsure of the change in her demeanor. "NOW, pet," she barked, and I quickly obeyed. Faster than I thought possible, she had my wrists and ankles tied down, leaving me completely helpless and exposed. She straddled my back and leaned down to kiss the back of my neck before tying the scarf around my eyes. Fuck. What had I gotten myself into? She climbed off and there was absolute silence for what felt like eternity. Then suddenly I felt a sharp slap on my ass, followed by another, and then another. I screamed, as much due to surprise as pain.

"If you scream again, I'll gag you. You hesitated when I gave you an order, and that's not acceptable." More spanking, even harder this time. I clenched my teeth to keep from screaming again. A few slaps later and then they stopped. I let out a little whimper. "Shhh, pet. It's over for now. Your pretty ass looks so hot and red. I can see my handprints all over it. A perfect canvas." I felt her crawl onto the bed and start caressing me, lifting my hips a little to wedge a pillow under them. My ass was now high in the air. Her tongue started running down my crack to my asshole and back up. She pulled my cheeks apart and sighed in contentment.

"Oh, your pretty little hole. It's so tightly closed right now, so afraid. We're going to see how much we can get it to open, aren't we? It'll take time, but let's see how far we can get today." I heard her spit and felt it land. Perfect bullseye. I was tingling in fear and anticipation. Her finger started to rub her saliva around, and she spit a few more times for good measure. She kept rubbing her finger around and around. I could feel a strange need building inside of me, and wiggled my ass the little I was able.

"What, do you want something, pet?

"Please…" I said, too embarrassed to admit the truth.

"Please what, pet? Use your words." Her finger continued to torment me, even starting to push at the entrance slightly a few times before circling around it again.

"Please… please put your finger in my ass." I knew I was blushing, and couldn't believe the words coming out of my mouth.

"You want my finger in your ass?"

"Yes." I was nearly panting at this point, every nerve strained.

"Yes what?" She slapped my ass again. I remembered our conversation earlier. "Yes ma'am," I replied, my humiliation complete.

"Good girl," she said, and pressed her finger deep in me. I moaned gutturally, loving the feeling. Somehow I had been missing this since our time last night and hadn't even known it. She didn't wait long this time to add the second finger, spitting a little more to make sure it was nice and wet. "Yes, that's it. Open up for me. Be my anal slut." Her voice was so fucking sexy, and made me want to take anything she gave me, just to hear her praise me more. A few minutes with two fingers, and she removed them both. I heard her grab something from the table, and suddenly felt something cool and slick being spread in and around my hole.

"We can't let you get hurt," she said, before pushing three well lubricated fingers slowly inside me. I gasped at the added stretch, but it wasn't painful, not really. I was surprised at how quickly the strangeness of it went away, and soon she was ramming all three in hard. My orgasm took me by surprise, and suddenly I was shaking all over.

"Oh god, pet. I can feel your orgasm in your ass. You're squeezing my fingers so tight." Elise was moaning with pleasure at the sensation. She waited until I was still before removing her fingers, her hands spreading my cheeks again.

"Oh yes, your first gape. It's so fucking beautiful, pet." She spit again, and this time I could feel her saliva slip inside of me. "Fuck yes," she said, burying her face in it. Her tongue pressed in much further than it did the night before, and I loved the feel of it licking inside of me. She kept at it for a long time before finally pulling back with a wet sound, and climbed off the bed. I could hear her moving around for a minute or two by the side of the bed, opening the box, but not being able to see had my imagination running wild. The bed dipped again as she climbed back on, and something hard and smooth was being pushed into the hole that her fingers had left behind.

At first it was easier to take than her fingers since it was so smooth, but she kept pushing and it kept getting bigger. I opened my mouth in protest, but before I could even say anything, she slapped my ass hard. "No, you don't tell me when to stop, pet. You'll take this, all of it, and you'll thank me for it," she said, still pushing and stretching me, making me burn, until I was about to scream regardless of punishment, when suddenly whatever it was popped in. I figured at that point that it must be some sort of anal plug, something I had seen before. The smaller part that was now stretching out my entrance was still bigger than her three fingers had been, but it seemed like nothing after I had experienced the rest of it.

"That's my good girl," she said, lovingly rubbing my ass cheeks, and then spreading them apart so she could see the plug better. "You've made such good progress so far today, and I'd hate for you to lose momentum while we explore other things, so think of this as a bookmark. I'm saving my spot so I can come back later. Now, what do you have to say?"

Oh god, was she really going to make me do it? A firm smack on my ass confirmed. "Thank you, m'am," I said. Her hands proceeded to untie me, but as soon as she had flipped me over onto my back, she tied me back down. Moving around at all with a giant plug in my ass was weird and uncomfortable, and I was glad to be still again. I felt her straddle my waist, her pussy hot and wet against my lower stomach. Then her lips were on mine, and I marveled at what an excellent kisser she was. She kissed me like she did everything else, alternatingly tender and rough, biting my tongue and my lips, then kissing away the pain. Sticking her tongue deep in my mouth, our teeth clashing together, then sucking my tongue into her own mouth. Soon I was panting with desire.

"Mmm... I think we need more oral practice, don't you?" She moved around again and suddenly her dripping pussy was on my face. I immediately stuck out my tongue to taste her, and as I did, I felt her tongue dip into my folds as well. I moaned into her at the visual that was playing through my head, and she rewarded the vibrations by grinding into my mouth. Her tongue was relentless on my clit as she stuck two fingers inside of me. Somehow they felt bigger than usual, since my ass was filled so tightly below. I licked at her frantically, wishing I could move so I could pull her in tighter, and so I could ride her fingers deeper, but I was completely immobile. We kept at it, both crazed with lust, her juices streaming down my throat and down the sides of my face. She was sucking hard on my clit, then licking down to my fingers and back. A few times she removed her fingers and I could hear her suck on them with delight before putting them back to fuck me harder. I made my tongue as stiff as possible and jammed it into her creamy hole as deep as I could. Suddenly, we were both exploding, screaming each other's names. Her cum was drowning me, even rushing down my nostrils. I coughed and gagged, but didn't turn my head, desperate to get as much of her as possible. We rode it out, and she collapsed on the bed beside me, panting. She then quickly moved again and crushed her lips into mine, our juices combining as we traded them back and forth across our tongues, until she let them all flow down in my mouth.

"Swallow us, pet." I instantly obeyed, feeling them slide down my throat. I felt hands remove my blindfold and looked up to see her beautiful face rising over mine, shiny with the evidence of what had just happened. She smiled down and kissed me gently, her hand stroking through my hair.

"Maxx," she said, admiration and affection shining through her eyes. "Will you be my girlfriend?"

I laughed. "I would love to be your girlfriend, Elise." She smiled with delight and kissed me again.

"There's just one more thing I need to do with you, just to confirm that you really are the girl of my dreams." Elise said this with a slightly concerned look on her face.

"Seriously, this again? I have loved everything. All of it." I was almost offended at this point. What did I have to do to prove to her that I could be every bit as nasty as she was? "Just name it, and we'll do it."

"I'd prefer to just do it, without discussion. The only thing I'll say is that I'll be disappointed if you waste a single drop." Elise moved around until she was straddling my face, her pussy just a few tantalizing inches out of reach.

"Keep your mouth open, pet," she said, staring down into my eyes as she started playing with herself above my lips. I opened my mouth in anticipation, remembering how delicious and juicy her orgasms had been. Her fingers were rubbing her clitoris, then plunging deep into her hole, back and forth, over and over, faster and faster. I watched in fascination as she became wetter and wetter before my very eyes. Soon, a few drops started to fall onto my tongue. I didn't dare swallow, for fear that I'd waste the next one. Instead, I felt them slide down to the back of my tongue. Even though I wasn't being touched in any way, I could feel my own orgasm building, thanks to the erotic show happening in front of me. This woman was the fucking hottest creature I had ever encountered. Her fingers were moving at a furious pace now, her pussy swollen, her clit engorged.

"Nod if you're ready to drink me, pet." Her eyes were wild with excitement and I barely nodded, not wanting to move my mouth too far. With a wild scream, she gave her pussy a strong slap, and lowered her hips until her mound was cradled in my mouth. I started sucking frantically at the flood of juices. After a few seconds, I suddenly realized that not only was she gushing more than anyone possibly could, the liquid had become thin and changed flavor. Then, reality hit. She was pissing into my mouth. Even as my eyes widened with shock, she reached down with both hands and pulled my face so tight into her crotch that I couldn't breath. I had no choice but to frantically swallow her hot urine, otherwise I'd drown. She was grinding back and forth,

10

using on my nose against her clit to build towards another orgasm. She screamed and came again, the piss dwindling even as more cum filled my mouth. The transition was incredibly unexpected, and then, to my absolute embarrassment, I felt myself start to cum.

I was cumming from being used as a combination sex toy and human toilet. I could feel my cheeks flush with shame even as I moaned into her pussy, swallowing the final drops. Her hips stopped moving, and we were both still. After another moment, she unsteadily climbed off my face and laid down beside me.

I didn't know what to say. I didn't know how to process what had just happened. I really didn't know how to process the fact that, while part of me was disgusted... The rest of me was wondering how soon we could do it again.

"Dream girl," Elise whispered in my ear as she snuggled into my side, and we both fell asleep from sheer exhaustion.

Galate:
Lesbian DP with a Married Woman
Maxx Harper

Eleanor was only a few years older than me, but had secured everything I now desired at a much earlier age. The thirty-five-year old woman was long married, her only child and daughter was attending college, and her husband was the chief of police.

Me? Thirty two, tragically single for longer than I cared to admit, a mere private investigator, and longing more and more to settle down with another woman. Maybe even adopt a kid or two. I've always entertained the thought of having my own someday, but mother insisted I would need a man for that.

I'm not that desperate.

"Sunbae?"

I felt my heart skip a beat at her soft, questing tone. When we first met online, she called me "senpai," a Japanese term many anime loving fans; the normal folks refer to them as weebs. But with me being Korean and not at all into Japanese animation, I jokingly insisted on her using sunbae, the Korean alternative. In turn, I affectionately designate her as my "hoobae," or "kouhai," as the anime fans would say.

"I'm in here, El." I poked my head out of the kitchen, a bottle of strawberry cream liqueur in one hand, two glasses clutched in the other. This was Eleanor's first time in my small and Spartan studio apartment. I think she took well to my Georgia O'Keefe painting. It was a gift from a very generous client.

"Sunbae, your apartment is so..." She paused, raising a thin, brown finger to tap at her upper lip. Cozy? Barren? Lonely? There was a reason I was iffy on bringing women home with me. Just a peek into my sad and pathetic life would be enough to make any wild squirter drier than the Sahara desert. "It's cute."

I groaned inwardly, but kept a smile on my face. Unless I made a colossal mishap, tonight was a sure thing. Eleanor was exploring her sexuality for the first time, and after much looking around, she'd come across me. Was I enthused about seeing a married woman? Not really. I may be anxious for human contact, but I also long for the romantic side of it. I want to be wooed and made to feel special, but with the perk of being fucked senseless. The simple stuff in life.

There was a soft clacking sound as the ice in the glasses rattled around with my every step. "It's nowhere near as cute as you, however." If it were anyone else but

Eleanor, I would be kicking myself for saying something so juvenile. But the other woman was oddly amused with my clumsy flirting; drawn to it, it seemed like. I could tell she wanted me as badly as I needed her. When we sat down on the couch together, she leaned a little into me, her hand resting against my inner thigh.

My hands trembled slightly as I poured the liquor. I wondered if she could feel my excitement, if it were outwardly notable like a man's. To keep myself focused, I began to blurt out the first thing in my head. "It's tequila, and tastes best chilled. I like to swirl my ice around to help speed up the effect." Her hand initially paused at the sound of my voice, but slowly returned to stroking my thigh. This was one of those times I regretted not wearing a skirt, but would she be so bold to keep this up if I were? I couldn't see her doing so.

"Sunbae is also very cute," she whispered, directly into my ear. I felt a chill run down my spine.

"You can just call me Danbi when we're alone." My voice was low, mirroring her husky undertones. I wanted to set the bottle down, throw her back onto the couch, and claim her mouth with my own. I wanted to make her forget about her husband for the night, taste her, explore her...

When I felt her lips caress my ear and kiss down my neck, my body betrayed me and let loose a soft

14

whimper. The whimper turned into a moan when teeth and tongue teased the flesh on my neck. "Danbi sunbae..." My hand squeezed around the bottle as I felt her suckling at my neck.

"D-don't you want your drink?" Shit. Why did I have to say that? "I mean." The ministrations on my neck ended, albeit with some hesitation.

I forced myself to confront those big old baby blues, and the caramel skin surrounding them. "Are you nervous?"

"Aren't you," I fired back. "It's your first time with a woman, isn't it?"

It was subtle, but I swear her cheeks grew darker. "Yes. But you looked really tense." Did I? I wonder why. "It helps when Liam is not in the mood."

I cringed. Liam. I tried to pretend the man did not exist most days, which was easier to do when I refused to name him. But Eleanor always found a way to remind me. "Well, I'm not Liam." I immediately regretted my choice of words when she flinched back. "I'm sorry."

"No...It's fine." She'd pulled back a little, blue eyes half-lidded and demurely facing the coffee table.

"I just...You always bring him up like this. I can't relax when you do." This was the problem with dating a taken woman. I was not that into the polyamory scene, but

Eleanor was special. I greatly enjoyed her presence, and could see myself falling for her completely if the circumstances were different. She was kind, affectionate, a little ditzy and hedonistic, but oh so endearing.

And after finishing half my drink, my mind was in a better state to acknowledge her curvaceous body, the full breasts, and the deceptively youthful appearance granted to her with her mixed heritage. Based on how she was now nuzzling against me, I think the tequila was getting to her as well.

The shy hand on my thigh traveled to the side, and slid against my groin. My knees twitched and my hips gently bucked. Her hand felt warm against the poor barrier of fabric keeping her out. I bit down on my lower lip when her fingers shifted, rubbing at the aroused crevice beneath. I placed a hand on her wrist, and guided it upwards, under my shirt but outside of my bra. I felt Eleanor's breath on my neck, rapid with excitement.

A moan of raw excitement was muffled with our lips. Eleanor was timid in the beginning, only pawing at my breast before dipping into my bra and seizing a warm mound. I could feel her other hand stroking between my legs, and in my blind state of arousal, I undid my zipped pants to provide her entry. Meanwhile, my hands were busy roaming her body.

I was less eager to move on to the main event, more content to explore and taste her at my leisure. I gently pushed her back onto the couch, ignoring my body's desperate demand for the caressing to resume, to find a release. But I wanted Eleanor. I wanted her here and now.

"Sunbae!" She gazed up at me, plump lips in a pout. What? Had I gone too far? No. Her hand was tugging at my wrist, plunging it beneath her breast. "Sunbae." I traced my hand around to her back, pressing my fingers against her warm skin. With one fluid motion, I seized the fabric behind her and pulled the shirt up and off. Large breasts in a pastel pink bra awaited me, and I wasted no time in pulling it off.

Eleanor whimpered and squirmed as I cupped her ample breasts in my small hands. They were perfect for stimulating her hardening nipples; palms or thumbs, it did not matter. They were clearly sensitive to the touch, more than what I've seen from experience. I could damn near smell Eleanor's pussy juices, and every cry or moan from her made me wetter and wetter. "Sunbae," she whined.

I could feel her getting impatient, but my only response was to pinch and tweak her now fully erect nipples. I lowered my head to her chest, kissed and nipped at everything but her breasts. Eleanor's legs shifted uneasily, reduced to a frustrated tremble when my questing hand slipped up her skirt. Once my hand made contact with the tell tale prick of pubic hair, and what felt like her dripping wet pussy, I ran my tongue under the curve of a heavy breath.

A firm hand pressed against the back of my head, bringing my face deeper into her bosom. I complied and kissed the hard nipple just above my nose. My fingers were gently rubbing at the warm mound at my hand, swiping down first to collect a sliver of her juices, and swinging up to tease her clit outside of her lips. My mouth latched onto the nipple and suckled on it like a hungry babe.

Having more than enough of my teasing by now, El spread her legs apart. Suddenly my hand was not teasing her outer lips, but sliding in her juices and overcome with an intense warmth. "Yes," she urged on. I slipped a single finger inside, gauging her reaction. Eleanor's hips rose and moved against my finger, nearly swallowing it whole. She was so wet and hot, but at the same time threatening to clamp down if I continued to tease her.

She grunted in dissatisfaction when I removed my finger, but perked up again when I kissed my way down to her belly. Her skirt had been removed at some point, so that she lied completely naked before me. Seeing the woman in such a state made my heart pound faster. I kissed and licked at her inner thighs, only stopping when she impatiently pushed my head between her lips. I gladly kissed her clit, an action that elicited a soft gasp of surprise from her.

The fingers entangled in my hair brought my face closer, enmeshed with her heat and wetness. I ran my tongue along her slit, occasionally targeting her clit until her stream of moans grew consistent, mounting. My tongue easily made its way into her soaked pussy, twirling around once it could go no further. Her hand pulled my head back and forth, to the point where I was flat out tongue fucking her.

I retook control so that I could suck on her clit and finger her at the same time, first with one finger, but working my way up to three. My pinky finger, slick with her juices, found her asshole and eased its way in. Eleanor was calling my name at this point, and clutching so hard to my head that I thought it would crumble under the pressure. "Just like that. Right there. Yes." She repeated this several times, interrupting her tempo at times to squeeze in a soft moan or squeal. "F-fuck me," she demanded.

I could do that, even mimic what she was used to. It required moving my head, however; into her inner thigh to catch a few breaths. My hand kept going, even as my other moved to the underside of the couch, where a small box sat. On top of the box was my strap-on and an assortment of toys I had stealthily prepared for tonight.

With the strap on perched on El's soft belly, I went through the motions of shedding the last of my clothing.

"Danbi, is--"

"You want to be fucked or not?" My tone hinted that I may be so inclined to drop the toy and continue hand fucking her, but that little quiver of her lip told me what she wanted. "Okay then. Lift your hips..." Eleanor tilted her hips and spread her legs, one thrown over the couch, other stretched out to the floor. Her pussy appeared to be slightly pulsating, hints of juice trickling into the crack of her ass. "Play with yourself," I commanded. I was beyond horny and had not focused on my own pleasure yet.

"O-oh. Like this?" Her dark skin turned a shade darker in timidity, but El ran the fingers of one hand along her glistening mound. I reached between my legs, stroking my clit and inner pussy lips in a similar motion.

"Yeah. Just like that. Touch your breasts, too." I ran my tongue over my lip, watching her shyly slide her middle finger knuckle deep into her pussy. She tugged and fumbled with her nipples until she found that sweet spot. "Just like that." I had two fingers inside my cunt by now, my thumb brushing against my clit with each jerk. When my pussy started to grow tight and tug at my fingers, I inserted the vibrating end of the dildo into me, and strapped on. Jutting out from a crotch was a large, purple dildo, vibrating with equal amounts of power as the smaller end inside of me. "Come here."

El did not need to be told twice. She shuffled closer to me, fingers used to spread her pussy lips as wide as possible, hips turned upwards and waiting in anticipation. "Sunbae, it's so big." Around eight inches, in fact. There was a much smaller dildo beneath the main one, for anal purposes. I was going to plug both holes if possible.

I entered her carefully and slowly, pausing when she tensed up, and applying full pressure once her legs were locked around my waist and her eyes unfocused. A soft grunt and her teased asshole was being stimulated by the smaller dong. With a strong pump of my hips, I plunged deep inside of her. The throaty moan in my ear only encouraged me to thrust harder and faster. Every time I moved my hips, the vibrating dildo inside me shifted and rubbed hard against my clit.

"El," I whispered into her ear. It felt so good that I feared I would cum early. I pressed my mouth against hers, kissing her hard and entangling our tongues together. Eleanor sucked hungrily at my lips and tongue, nipping at the former as my movements became stronger and bucked her body back and forth. I seized one of her nipples in my hand, turning, pinching, and rubbing it in my frustration.

"Danbi, it feels so good." Her eyes were wild, like an animal in heat. She even clawed at my back like one, surely drawing blood but I was not going to let a little thing like pain get in my way. I pinched one of her nipples, hard. She threw her head back, teeth pinning a plump lip in place. Her nails dug deeper into my back. She didn't need to say it, because I could feel it, too. The way her body seized up, she was on the edge and ready for release.

I increased my tempo, this time with one hand rubbing her clit. Her legs twitched in reaction as I touched down on that sweet spot, both inside and outside. Desperate for a release myself, I finally gave in to the mounting pleasure. We came simultaneously, though it was obvious she got much more out of it than I did.

El was reduced to a sweating, breathless bundle, unable to move for at least ten minutes. I know this because I was collapsed on top of her for just as long, fatigued from the strain of using the strap on. It was a good excuse for us to cuddle and kiss, at least. She was warm and flushed all over, so I could only imagine how I looked, with my pale skin.

After a short time, Eleanor broke the silence. "Sunbae, can we do it again? Liam never can..." I stared back at her, too caught up in my own daze to bring up our "No Liam" rule, but my pussy's insistent throbbing pushed those thoughts aside. "Please?" I sucked on her lower lip

in agreement. We had the entire night to ourselves,
after all.

Hot Honey Lesbians
By Alexia Engles

Honey Cuts Salon was on the better end of town and the clientele was middle class urban dwellers. Brandy and Mia were roommates and they both worked at the salon. The fact that their living together was a secret from the world is because Mia is the former lover of the salon owner.

Leah was in her late thirties and her sweet berries were aged to perfection. She often wore light colors and whites and kept her hair a beautiful bleach blonde. She was the typical story of successful small business owner with a Jaguar and under paid employees. Leah had a real knack for using money and sex to manipulate her lovers, workers, and friends. Her body was a perfect ten and her pussy showed lovely clit lips which on sight made most women fall to their knees and lick. This was the case with Mia but since Brandy was still kind of new at the salon, Leah hadn't used her shaved and flowering muff to trance her, yet.

Most every young salon worker's dream is to own their own business and live by their own terms. Leah set a beautiful example of a dream any woman would want to live. Money, cars, and controlling interest on the twats of her choice. A revolving door of dreamers, broken dreams, and gash spread wide at Honey Cuts Salon.

There were three rooms at the salon and one would say the salon was average size. There was the main lobby and salon area, a large bathroom and Leah's office. In the unisex bathroom was a large wooden changing table which Leah had built strong enough to support the weight of two people, much like a large massage table. The toilet had its own enclosure within the bathroom, and there was a pedestal sink. It was after 9 pm and the salon was closed, two stylists, Daphne and Sophia have locked the bathroom door and are taking full advantage of the installed fuck table.

Daphne's red hair was streaked light blonde and her naked body was tan and open to Sophia's tongue in her savory pussy. Sophia leaned against the table and tried to work her finger into Daphne's barely fucked asshole. Daphne moaned quietly and spread wider to allow more room for fingers and Sophia's tongue. Sophia was using a dominant thrust into the ass and slurping on the twat lips. The sound was similar to beating eggs with a whisk and Daphne fought to control her multiple orgasms which seemed to fire in response to each bit and nibble of the clit.

One of the rules of the fuck room was to clean up after secretions. These two hot honey pies really jizzed-up the fuck table and it was during the cleanup that they discussed and agreed that there was something more to the relationship between Brandy and Mia. Sophia wanted to prove Brandy and Mia are in bed together so Leah will favor her over Mia for a summer publicity campaign which involved a photo shoot. All the stylists knew that if you did publicity work with Leah then there was a good chance to lick Leah's golden bean. Sophia knew that if she had the chance to slobber Leah's cooter then other opportunities and better wages were sure to come. Sophia knew Leah was a player so her plan was to have hot lesbian sex and give Leah whatever she wanted.

Meanwhile, back at Mia and Brandy's apartment, it is erotic toy night. Mia was never fond of clothes so lying naked on the sofa and taking vibrators, dildos, and anal beads from Brandy was pure ecstasy. One of Brandy's favorite parts of this live-in fuck arrangement, and being a woman lover, was the taste, smell and feeling of rubbing her face and nose on a sweet vagina and anus. The long tender legs of a woman, soft skin, fresh hair, sensitivity and soft anal pleasures. Outside a party in college and in the back of an SUV, Brandy had been fucked up her ass by a guy and she remembered that it was good but really hurt. She never had this problem with Mia. It was Brandy's turn to spread wide and get worked on by her sultry, steamy, swollen chested lover. Mia licked the tender flaps and creases of Brandy's perfectly formed asshole and slowly began to let saliva buildup. First her fingertips and then the blue walnut size beads squished pass the folds and created a gush of saliva and ass cum which allowed the beads easy in-and-out action.

Mia continued to flick Brandy's pussy lips with her tongue. Brandy was bent over the couch and Mia moved under her box like a mechanic under a station wagon. Mia pounded the beads up Brandy's ass and then pulled them out abruptly just to jam them in again and again. Brandy twerked her hips and fucked the beads into her ass and screwed her twat into Mia's face. Mia was in a full sipping pucker with her mouth on Brandy's gap as tasty juices flowed from her clam and fanny.

When Mia arrived at work the next day, she was told by Daphne that Leah wanted to see her in the office immediately. Mia was ready, now was the time to tell Leah what was really going on between Brandy and wanting to start their own business. At that point, she realized that Sophia must be in on this and that it was a play on the photo shoot opportunity. Mia didn't care anymore because she loved Brandy and just wanted to be out of the clutches of Honey Cuts Salon and Leah's perfect pussy.

That's right, "the perfect pussy!" Mia began to panic what would she do when Leah pushes her skirt aside and flashes the majestic muffin that so many women crave to savor. The irresistible rump of opportunity, with just a lick, Leah would surely fund Mia's own salon, and the thought was tempting. She remembered that fucking Leah's flawless honeypot had strings attached and leaving this controlling life style was her best choice to advance her life. Luckily she had a good partner like Brandy to help guide her away from Leah's grasp.

Before the office door locked, Mia and Leah were feverishly tongue kissing and peeling each other's clothes off. Mia re-buttoned her blouse and skirt but kept disrobing Leah. Leah was now topless and skirt up with Mia's face plowing into her openings. With her mouth still on Leah's asshole, and finger in the cabbage, Mia used the other hand to pull an extremely large, massive black dildo from her bag. Mia went back to tonguing Leah's face and she slammed the enormous dildo up against Leah's golden pussy bean. Leah yelped and Mia quieted her with more passionate kissing.

From the salon area, Daphne heard the yelp and realized Leah is getting her box cleaned. She begins to feel jealous and upset that Mia is getting her opportunities filled. Behind the office walls, it is Leah being filled, bent over the desk and slammed repeatedly by Mia's massive rubber dildo. Slamming Leah's supple rear, Mia herself began to cum in her mini skirt. She knew this was the end. That was her final fuck to set things straight between her and Leah. Leah moaned in heat while Mia worked her fist into Leah's gushing meat pocket with the

28

slamming of the giant black dildo continually in her ass. Leah's shaven pussy and tender soft lips were spread wide like a stuffed turkey as her clit bean bulged bright pink with the juice of the Earth's sweetest nectar.

Still dressed, Mia gave her fist and the dildo a final slam into Leah. Leah lay across her desk with her cooze and cunt bean twitching with flowing white and clear cum. Mia got down on her knees and from behind licked Leah from bean to asshole. The sweet-sweet taste of this magnificent woman brought the essence of lavender and posies. Mia couldn't resist a second lick, so she guzzled Leah's holes one last time then left the office with the door open and Leah lying in euphoria. "Tell Sophia, she could have the photo shoot, bitch," Mia smacked Daphne's bottom on the way out and Brandy nor Mia were never seen by the Honey Cuts crew again.

Daphne, on the other hand, took her opportunity to get spotlighted for the photo shoot by jumping in where Mia left off. Bang, Bang, Bang! Leah's bean was blasted hours more with the gigantic black dong when Daphne found her open holes still oozing in the office. Leah was limp but smiling as Daphne took order at Honey Cuts Salon. The once dominant Leah was fucked into submission and she was forever different with the way she treated her employees. She still ruled with a golden bean but all stylists were considered equal partners in the business. Let's just say this increased the amount her ladies craved her perfect ass and twat. The colossal black dildo became a permanent fixture and a daily routine for the fun loving, hot honey lesbians.

Eating out the College Dean: A Student's First Lesbian Experience

By Krista Collar

The sound of my sandals, echoed through the hall of the empty Administration building of the University. Nervousness coursed through my trembling body as I approached my final destination. I had no idea why I was called to report to the Dean's office, but this was my first visit since I began attending three years ago.

Apparently we had a new Dean. Her name is Vivian Williams, and is known to be fierce and intimidating. She attended a prestigious University, where she earned her Doctoral degree in Astrophysics, which is what I am studying as well. She was now head of the Physics department, and apparently was dismissing students who she did not see fit for this rigorous program.

My breathing hitched as I stand in front of the oak door that had her name printed quite clearly on the front. I raised my knuckles to the wood, and knocked very lightly. I nervously tugged at my sweater, unsure if she was going to kick me out of her program or not. I've worked too hard and long to fail now. It simply was not an option for me at this point.

The door immediately swung open, as the most attractive woman I've ever seen peers down at me with a serious glare. "Well don't just stand there. Come in!" she snapped, causing me to hightail it inside of her office.

Now, I am only a twenty-four year old and have never been in a relationship. I have also never found other women as sexually appealing, but watching Dr. Williams as she elegantly maneuvered her way around the room, caused a spark of attraction within me.

She took a seat in a large leather chair and rested her elbows on her grand desk. Her bright emerald eyes ignited an inner fire, and her shoulder length blonde hair looked like silk that makes me want to run my fingers through it. She didn't appear to be older than forty, but she looked absolutely fabulous. She was hiding a rocking body under her clothes.

"Let us get down to business, shall we?" she reached in her cabinet and set down a manila folder that appears to be my file. "I wanted to discuss a few things with you." She scanned down my body slowly, as if she were checking me out. *She can't be.*

"What is that you wanted to discuss, Dr. Williams?" I asked unsurely, placing a strand of my brunette hair behind my ear. She licked her lips in response. I squeezed my legs shut, attempting to stop the wetness that was pooling out of me, but I was failing rather miserably.

"I have been reading your file," she paused, giving me another glance with her darkened eyes. "I must say that I am rather impressed with your exceptional credentials, Miss Waters."

I finally released the long breath that I had been holding. Her eyes were swirling with what seemed like lust and desire. Surely it couldn't be towards me. She's probably married with a handsome husband and beautiful children. But when I flickered my eyes to her ring finger, it's bare.

"Thank you, Dr. Williams. What can I say? I am a nerd for Astrophysics." I laughed a little, trying to put my mind at ease. But I knew all too well that I was hungry for her.

"As you know, Astrophysics is a rather time consuming program." She leaned forward, the crevices of her breasts exposing themselves in my direction. "I hope your *boyfriend* is supportive." She said, making me think that she is somehow testing me.

"That's not an issue." I immediately responded. Her brow arched in curiosity. "I don't have a boyfriend, or any significant other for that matter." A part of me wanted her to know how desperately single I was. God, she was fucking sexy as hell.

"Oh," she said.

I watch as she gracefully rose from her chair and swayed her hips as she positioned herself behind me. Her hand reached around to cup my chin. I felt the sparks of electricity as her skin touched mine, and I instantly became turned on. She tilted my head back, so that I was looking into her dark eyes.

My lips parted open so that I could allow more air to enter my lungs. My heart was racing like a raging metronome. When I least expected it, her lips came crashing down onto mine. A wave of desire and sensuality washed over me like a blazing wildfire in a dry forest. The only way to put it out was to have her, and have her immediately.

As our lips collided in a passionate love affair, I began to lose myself in her, and I could feel her losing herself in me. Her fingers wrapped themselves securely in my wavy hair as she pulled me back even further to reach optimum contact. Her scent was a mixture of vanilla and lavender that caressed my nostrils like a wicked temptress. I craved her in every way possible.

"Have you ever been with a woman?" she asked, pulling away from me, which causes me to silently pout in response.

"No." I answer honestly. "But I want you." As soon as those words left my mouth, I pulled her head down with my small hand and immersed myself in her touch as our tongues clashed in pure desire.

"Let me show you a world of pleasure, Marina." She whispered seductively in my ear. A series of tingly shivers ran down my spine from her delicious hot breath. "I want you just as badly."

Dr. Williams stood before me with an aura of confidence that radiated from her body. I subconsciously licked my lips that craved to touch hers. Her thumb rested on my lower lip and she leaned down, studying every inch of my face. She slowly produced a wicked grin that makes my panties drenched.

She placed her hands on the sides of my sweater, and carefully lifted it over my head, and tossed it on the Persian rug below us. Her right hand cupped my breast, kneading and massaging it firmly. I released a small moan, letting her know that her attention is much appreciated.

Vivian pulled me up from my seat, wrapping her lean arms around my small waist. Her hand cupped the back of my neck as our tongues battled in a sensuous manner. She tasted like sweet honey, and my addiction for her grew even stronger than before. I was betting that she'd taste even better in *other* areas.

She guided me over to her large desk, and sits me atop of it. I wrapped my legs around her waist as I began to grind myself against her. Her fingers unclamped my noir-laced bra, allowing it to fall freely. Her index finger and thumb rolled and tugged at my swollen nipples. I arched my neck back and moaned out in delight.

Her lips began to place wet kisses along my jawline and down towards the curve of my neck. Her tongue licked and teased an area near my collarbone that creates a euphoric burning sensation. I ran my fingers through her blonde silky hair, and I heard her groan in response. My hands then found their way to the buttons of her white dress top, and I unbuttoned them fast and furiously.

"Someone is hot and bothered." She smirked at me, while I literally ripped the shirt from her body, revealing a perfect set of toned abs and perky breasts.

I leaned forward and placed my mouth over the soft material of her bra, sucking her hard peak that lies underneath. Her hands rested on my hips, while I continued to rub myself against her. She closed her eyes and leans her head back with parted lips. Her expression of pleasure was the most erotic sight that I have ever seen.

Slipping her bra off, my mouth reconnected with the warm flesh of her plump breast. I grasped the other with my hand as my tongue swirled around her areola. She moaned in elation as I teased her pink bud between the tips of my teeth.

Suddenly, she pushed me back on the desk so that I was now lying in front of her. She undid the button to my jeans, and slipped them off of me. She looked into my eyes with much intensity and a sexual hunger. I could probably have had an orgasm just by looking at her.

I felt my panties being guided down my legs as her fingernails scraped gently against my pale skin. Shivers and tingles ran wild through my body. Her hands pried my thighs apart, and I felt slightly embarrassed because I know that my pussy was about as drenched as Niagra Falls, but by the expression on her face, I could tell that she was pleased.

As she leaned over to kiss me again, I gasped when I felt her finger playing between my silky folds. My hips involuntarily moved against her finger, and when she noticed this, she slipped her finger into my very soaked aperture. Immediately, she found my sensitive spot and began to rub against it ferociously.

I cried out in pleasure from the overwhelming sensations. She pulled back to watch me, adding in another finger. Vivian Williams is a master at foreplay, and I bet that this wasn't her first lesbian encounter. No one is *this* good.

"Oh, yes! Dr. Williams!" I screamed out her name as I feel myself tightening around her fingers.

Her thumb circled around my clit to stimulate my nerves even further than before. I never thought that it was possible to experience such an intense sensation. My eyes rolled back into my head as I exploded around her fingers. My body shook and trembled from the aftershocks. I can honestly say that was the best release that I've ever had.

"Now it's my turn." I said with a sudden boost of confidence.

Vivian arched her brow with curiosity. I hopped off of the desk, still naked. I guided her onto the desk and laid her down like she did with me. I hitched her skirt up over her knees and around her upper thighs. I intertwined my fingers around the side strings of her thong on pull them off of her.

I sat down on my knees, and spread her legs as wide as possible, discovering her rather impressive flexibility. She shuttered from my hot breath that is dangerously close to her glistening cunt. She tangled her fingers in my hair as I connected the tip of my tongue to her throbbing cleft. I began tracing light patterns around her tasty form, just to get myself started.

When I started to feel more comfortable with my performance, my tongue danced over her with more pressure and intensity as I swirled it around in circles. I then flickered up and down rapidly to increase her pleasure. Her hands tightened in my hair, as she moaned uncontrollably.

I moved myself lower, tasting more of her delicious juices. She was even sweeter than I previously imagined, and she was almost too addicting. My tongue entered her vagina slowly, but soon I pushed it in as far as it could go, exploring her treasured cave. I guided myself back up so that I was fiercely stimulating her clit with my tongue once more.

She began to stiffen as a pool of wetness escaped her pussy. I inwardly smiled in all my glory, satisfied that I was able to please her as much as she did me. By the time I stood back up, we were both heavily out of breath. The office smelled of perfume and sex, creating an intoxicating scent.

We both put our clothes back on, stealing glances at each other. She gave me a warm smile, as I produced one in return. I can't stop thinking about our recent escapade.

"Come see me next week, Miss Waters. Thank you for
your... *time.*"

While the Husband Is Away, the Girls Will Play: I'm Having an Affair with My Lesbian Neighbor

By: L.J. Harper

I was in my room one evening getting ready for bed when all of the sudden, the power went out. I grabbed a candle and lit it. I could just hardly see the door to my room open. I asked, "Who's there?" I heard no reply, and then all of the sudden a pair of thin arms grabbed me.

I struggled to get away until I heard her voice, "I got you!" It was Jenna, my neighbor; she must have shut the power off downstairs. Jenna and I had a secret relationship. Whenever my husband was gone on business, she would come over and have some fun with me. Jenna's husband had died a few years back and ever since then she hasn't been with a man, but she has been with a few women. As Jenna pushed me onto the floor I could see her grin in the candlelight. I noticed her chest bulging out of her daughter's shirt, as well. It was so hot; I knew she wasn't wearing a bra.

As she pinned me to the ground she asked, "Do you want me?"

"Yes!"

She replied," I can't hear you!"

So, I screamed, "Yes, god yes! Jenna, make me beg!"

Jenna then slowly unbuttoned my nightgown until my breasts were just barely showing. She kissed me while she pinched my nipples. She tugged at them hard; it hurt, but also felt kind of nice. She then yanked off my nightgown and started sucking one of my nipples. I just laid there while she turned me on. She switched her mouth and hands back between each of my tits. She then stood up and sat on my chest. She told me to take off her thong with my mouth, I followed my orders. Then she said, "Suck on the thong, open up your mouth and suck on it." I did it tasted so good I could taste all of her juices. Jenna asked," Do you like that? Those are my daughters." I couldn't believe Jenna had taken her daughters underwear and that they were in my mouth, but I didn't care it just made me wetter.

As I lay there, she made me put the thong on over my head and then Jenna proceeded to sit on my face. I ate her out for so long. Her pussy was fucking my tongue. I couldn't describe the feeling; I never wanted it to end. Jenna just moaned while I ate her out; she loved it! Eventually she sat up and returned the favor. Her tongue slowly went from my mouth down to my dripping wet cunt. I wanted her so bad but she made me squirm and beg for it. Jenna circled her tongue around my pussy while I lay there in anticipation. She finally touched it and licked it a few times before sucking on my clit. She sucked on that bad girl for a good while. She flicked her tongue and fingered me real well.

I was about to about to cum and then she started giving me a rim job. I had never had that experience before; I felt so alive! She swirled her tongue in little circles around my tight asshole. She then sat me up on all fours and stuck a finger in my ass. It was a strange tight feeling but it started feeling really good. Then Jenna put two fingers in my pussy and one in my ass, and started going in and out very slowly. I was in heaven. I was in love with Jenna. I wanted her so bad. I started cumming. My pussy was like a waterfall; I knew it would stain my carpet but I didn't care. I told Jenna it was amazing and that I wanted to do the same to her. Jenna said I could but she made me lick up my spill on the floor first. It made me feel disgusting.

I started fingering Jenna's ass. It wasn't as tight as mine; I could tell this was something she had enjoyed before. I stuck four fingers in there and wiggled them. Jenna told me to pump my fist into her, so I did. I got my entire fist in her ass and I started to feel like I was hurting Jenna, but it only made Jenna hornier. I pumped back and forth until she finally came all over the floor just like I had. I made her lick it up too, but my fist was in her ass the whole time.

Once I removed my hand, I kept staring at her asshole. It was so wide, so I told her to stick her ass in the air. I spread her cheeks apart and spit in her asshole. She thought it was so hot. I told her, "You think that's hot? Then watch this. Stay right there, don't more." I walked into the bathroom and peed in a small Dixie cup. I brought it back into the bedroom and pulled her cheeks apart again and slowly poured my hot piss down her ass. Jenna screamed.

She then squatted on top of me and relaxed her ass. All of my piss spilled from her onto my chest. I proceeded by eating Jenna out again while she began to eat me out too. We 69nd for the next hour and we both probably came 3 times. Once we were worn out we got in the bathtub to wash off. We scrubbed soap all over each other's breasts to ensure my husband would never find out about our affair, and especially about this particularly scandalous night.

Tied, Licked, and Strap On Anal for the Lesbian Executive

Krista Collar

Tasha looked up from her computer in the small cubicle as Serena walked by. Pretending like she was leaning over to pick up a stack of paperwork , she watched Serena's hips sway, as she walked toward her office, and imagined what she would look like as she held onto those hips as while she was fucking her. As Serena's office door shut, Tasha gave herself a mental shake, picked up the paper work and sat it on her desk.

Later that evening, as Tasha lay in her bed, she thought about her earlier fantasies and sighed. Serena was straight, she was pretty sure of it. And even if she wasn't there was no way she would ever be interested in her. She was just an administrative assistant and women like Serena, no matter how beautiful they were, didn't get to be top advertising executives by noticing people like her. Still, she couldn't stop thinking about the way Serena's hips swayed and how tight her ass was.

She started imaging what it would be like to meet Serena somewhere outside of work and take her home. She imagined slowly unbuttoning the green silk top Serena had been wearing today and sliding it down her bare arms. She imagined kissing and licking the swell of Serena's cleavage as she undid the black lace bra, that Tasha just knew, was underneath the top, and sucking Serena's nipple into her mouth and then flicking it with her tongue as she massaged that tight ass that had so captivated her earlier in the day.

Almost without realizing it, Tasha's hand slid up her T-shirt that she had put on to sleep in and started rubbing and plucking at her nipples. Her other hand slid down to skim through the neatly trimmed hair above her pussy, coming to rest on her clit. It was a good thing she had stopped wearing panties to bed since these fantasies about Serena had started. It was too easy to get herself hot and bothered just by thinking about what she wanted to do to Serena and panties were just an inconvenience.

Tasha started imaging the sounds that Serena would make as she shoved her down on the bed and pulled her black skirt down her legs taking her panties with it. And as she thought about forcing Serena's legs to stay open while she licked her clit and made her squirm, she started rubbing her clit faster and faster. Just as she imagined pushing her fingers deep inside Serena's hot, tight, very wet pussy and feeling it tighten around them she exploded, startling herself with the force of it.

After the shudders had subsided, Serena rolled onto her side, and put a pillow between her legs, tight up against her to help with the lingering pulses of the force of her orgasm. Irritated at herself for wanting someone she could never have, Tasha drifted off to sleep.

The next afternoon, Tasha kept a close eye on Serena's office door. She couldn't stop thinking about the force of her orgasm the night before, and every time she caught a glimpse of Serena she could feel the moisture between her legs start to build. Eventually, Serena's door opened and Tasha watched as she escorted her client out of the office. Even that small glimpse of Serena was enough to make her even wetter.

Tasha quickly got up and made her way to the restroom. She chose the last stall and slipped in, locked it behind her. Pulling her slacks down she sat on the toilet, and slid her fingers inside her pussy. If just seeing Serena could do this to her what would it be like to actually fuck her? She began to slide her fingers inside herself faster and faster, and to rub her clit with her other hand. She knew it wouldn't take long, that woman just had that effect on her.

Through the erotic haze, Tasha heard the bathroom door open, and Serena's sultry voice filter in as she said goodbye to someone on the phone. The few words Tasha heard Serena say, sent her over the edge and she bit her lip to keep from crying out.

Cleaning herself up, she let herself out of the stall and almost ran straight into Serena as she made her way to the sink to wash her hands.

"Sorry!" Tasha winced.

"No problem. Are you alright? You look a little flushed." Serena asked.

"I'm alright, just not feeling too well today." Tasha replied as she washed hands.

"You should take the rest of the day off then." Serena told her. "There will be some late nights in the next month, so we will need everyone at their best."

"I think I will take you up on that." Tasha answered. She didn't think that she could handle spending the rest of the day watching for Serena, and thanking the stars that today was Friday.

Tasha's doorbell rang and she got up off the couch, where she was putting her shoes on, to answer it. It was her two best friends, Tony and Beth.

"You ready to go?" Tony asked.

"Pretty much, just give me a couple more minutes." Tasha replied as she walked in her bedroom to grab her wallet and keys.

The three made their way downstairs, and into the waiting cab, "To Betty's, please" Tasha told the cab driver. Betty's was the local gay bar. Tasha had invited her friends out for a night of fun and to hopefully be able to find some nice little lesbian that she could work her frustrations off with.

As the three got to the bar, it was packed, and Tasha quickly made her way to the bar to get drinks for the three of them. After getting the drinks she returned to her friends and they started making their way through the club, looking to see if they knew anyone who was there. It wasn't long before Tony ran into an old "acquaintance" and was huddled up in the corner, talking to him and rubbing on him.

Tasha laughed, knowing that there was more rubbing than talking going on. "Never takes him long does it?" She leaned over and said Beth.

"No. Never. That man can get laid quicker than anyone I know. Hell, he will probably had fucked three guys up the ass in the bathroom by the time I have even started to talk to a girl." Beth shook her head, and looked around.

"Actually," she said and stopped walking, "I may have to amend that statement, I have been talking to a girl online, and it looks like she actually showed up tonight." Beth discreetly pointed to a girl standing at the second bar. "I'm afraid I am going to have to ditch you early too."

"No problem! Good luck." Tasha replied, as she leaned in to kiss her on the cheek.

Tasha continued wondering around the bar, stopping to chat with friends she knew, and refill her drink at the bar. As she did, she kept her eyes open and scanned the crowd for someone that looked good enough to eat, but wasn't having any luck. A few hours later, as she was coming out of the bathroom stall, she bumped into someone on her way to the sink.

"We really have to stop meeting this way." A familiar voice laughed, as Tasha's mouth dropped open.

"Wha... What are you doing here?" Tasha said as she skimmed her eyes up and down Serena, who was clothed in a tight fitting red blouse and short dark skirt.

"The same thing you are, I imagined. I'm surprised I haven't ran into you here before."

"Why is that?" Tasha asked as she finished washing her hands.

"Well, it is a little obvious which way you, umm swing, and this is the best gay bar in town. Besides I believe I may have seen you watching my ass a time or two." Serena shrugged.

At that Tasha blushed, but then took a good hard look at Serena's face.

"Oh, yeah? And why do you think that?" Tasha replied with a smirk.

"Are you denying it?"

"Why don't you let me show you how much I am denying it?" Tasha said, as she backed Serena into a stall and shut the door behind them.

She immediately started kissing Serena, and pushed her against the side of the stall.

"That's definitely not a denial." Serena breathed as Tasha started rubbing her tits.

"Come on," Tasha said dragging Serena out of the stall and the bathroom, and pulling her toward the front door.

"Where are we going?" Serena asked, as she tried to slow Tasha down, a little surprised at how forceful she was being.

Tasha turned, and pulled Serena to her, grinding her leg against Serena's pussy, "I have a lot of plans for you, we are going to my place, or yours if you prefer."

"Yours is fine" Serena replied, as Tasha led her outside and hailed a cab.

As soon as they stepped in to Tasha's apartment she pushed Serena against the door, and held her hands above her head, while she gave her a searing kiss. "The bedroom." She said and pulled Serena toward it.

After reaching the bedroom, Tasha threw Serena onto the bed and went to a drawer in her dresser. She pulled out two pieces of Japanese love rope, and dropped them on the bed, and started to climb onto it, straddling Serena who was propped on her elbows.

"What are those for?" Serena asked, eyeing the ropes.

"Well," Tasha said as she started skimming her hands over Serena's breasts. "I told you I had plans for you, and I don't want you to stop me until I have had a chance to enact them all."

"Mmmm, but you haven't told me what they are yet." Serena said in between deep breaths.

"You'll like it, I promise." Tasha said, as she peeled Serena's dress off over her head.

"No panties..," Tasha said taking in the black bra, and trimmed pussy of Serena, "Nice touch." And unsnapped her bra.

Tasha then stripped her own clothes off, and lay down on top of Serena, rubbing her nipples with one hand, while kissing and biting her neck. Serena moaned.

"Come on." Tasha said and pulled Serena up to the head board and starting tying her left hand to the wrought iron.

"Too tight?" she asked as she moved to the other side.

"No, No, it's just right." Serena said, trying to run her tongue along Tasha's stomach as she moved across her.

"None of that." Tasha stated. "Tonight is about my fantasies."

As soon as she was done tying her hands up Tasha settled herself between Serena's legs and gave her a very long kiss, shoving her tongue in her mouth and grinding her pussy against Serena's.

"You'll have to tell me when you can't take it anymore, I intend for this to be a very, very long night." Tasha told her as she started to move down Serena's body. Serena moaned.

"Oh and don't worry about screaming. The walls here have had that soundproofing insulation."

And with that Tasha put her mouth on one of Serena's breast and her hand on her other nipple. Serena started to squirm and reach for Tasha, but she couldn't with her hands tied. Tasha switched to the other breast and Serena struggled even harder.

"Oh god," she cried.

"We haven't even started yet." Tasha said and moved down to blow on Serena's pussy. It was already wet and dripping.

"Mmmm, I'm going to enjoy this," Tasha said as she settled herself between Serena's legs. Tasha put her palms against each one of Serena's legs and pushed them wide, and then buried her face in her pussy. Serena gasped and tried to squirm, but Tasha was holding her in place.

Tasha flicked her tongue along Serena's clit over and over again, holding her legs wide. After about ten minutes she moved down and flicked her tongue inside Serena a few times.

"Please," Serena begged, panting.

"Already can't take anymore?" Tasha chuckled. "Well, I'm not done yet and these are my fantasies remember." Letting one of Serena's legs go, she sat up and watched her face as she slid two fingers inside her.

"Serena moaned and arched her back, struggling against her ropes. "Do you know how wet this makes me?" Tasha asked. She reached down and put the same two fingers inside her pussy that had just been in Serena's. As she drew them out, she put them in Serena mouth and then leaned down to kiss her, while she ground against her.

54

Tasha leaned over and whispered in Serena's ear "I'm going to eat your cunt until you come and then I'm going to fuck you until you come, and then after that I'm going to bend you over and fuck you up the ass until you come. Those are my plans for you." Serena moaned and tried to rub her pussy against Tasha's some more, but Tasha was already moving down to lick her cunt, just like she had said.

Tasha spread Serena's legs again and this time when she started flicking her tongue on Serena's clit, she also shoved her fingers inside her roughly. Serena jumped and moaned. Tasha looked up and watched Serena's face as she fucked her with her fingers and saw how flushed it was. Looking back down she licked her clit over and over again, shoving her fingers inside her with the same rhythm.

"Oh, fuck!" Serena yelled and started screaming as she came on Tasha's face and squeezed her fingers.

After she stopped screaming, Tasha sat up. "Remember I'm not done with you yet." And she got up and went to the same drawer that she had pulled the rope out of. Tasha took something out of the drawer and snapped it around each leg. As she turned around, Serena saw the pink strap on that Tasha had put on and whimpered.

Tasha climbed back into bed and positioned herself between Serena's legs. "Let's see if I can fuck as good as a man. But I must say I have an advantage…" She leaned down and placed the strap on against Serena's clit and started licking her nipples.

Serena heard a click as Tasha looked up at her and said "Mine vibrates."

Tasha shifted and pushed the dildo inside Serena. Serena moaned and squirmed. Tasha sat up on her knees and pushed the dildo in and out, faster and faster, watching Serena's tits bounce as she fucked her harder and harder, and watched her squirm and moan. Tasha reached down and started rubbing on Serena's tits while she fucked her, and finally Serena shuttered and yelled.

"Oh God, I don't know that I can take anymore Tasha." Serena whispered when she could finally catch her breath.

"Just one more." Tasha said as she leaned down to kiss her. "Roll over."

Tasha help Serena roll over, and pushed her onto her knees. She started rubbing her hands up and down Serena's ass cheeks, and Serena started squirming again. Serena felt something slip inside her pussy and felt Tasha strap it around her legs. It was inside her and a point rested against her clit as well. After a second it started to vibrate. Serena shuddered and moaned.

"This is what I was thinking about doing when I was staring at your ass." Tasha said as she slowly pushed the dildo inside Serena's tight asshole.

"You tight, Never done this before?" Tasha asked and started to move.

"No." Serena breathed.

"Good." Tasha said and started to move faster and harder.

"Tell me how good it feels. Tell me that you like it. Beg me not to stop." Tasha demanded.

"I love it, it feel so fucking good. Don't stop Tasha… Don't stop." Serena yelled. Tasha started fucking her harder and faster, shuddering while she did it.

"Let go, Serena. Come for me. I don't know how long I can last."

"I'm coming. Oh shit. I'm fucking coming!" Serena said as she started to shudder.

Tasha shoved the dildo in Serena's ass one more time and pushed it hard against her, holding it in. She panted hard a few times, and then started screaming as she came, while gripping Serena's ass hard.

When she could finally moved, she eased the dildo out of Serena's ass, and reached down and took the other vibrator out of her pussy. Serena collapsed on the bed still breathing hard.

Tasha took the strap on off and sat it on the dresser and then ran her hand lightly up Serena's ass cheeks and back before moving to untie her. Serena rolled over and snuggled against her, as Tasha climbed into bed and pulled the sheets up over them.

"That was amazing." Serena murmured, as she drifted off to sleep.

"I've had a long time to fantasize about you, and have spent a long time staring at your ass at work." Tasha chuckled, before kissing her head and dropping off to sleep herself.

The next morning, Tasha woke up and tried to remember what had happened the night before, as it started to come back, she wasn't quite sure it was reality and not a really excellent fantasy. Then she heard the bathroom door open. Rolling over she watched Serena walk out of the bathroom and come sit down on the bed and start to get dressed from a pile of clothes she must have gathered while Tasha was still sleeping.

Tasha slid over and put an arm around Serena's naked waist, kissing her side. "Where are you going?" She asked.

"I have to go and get ready for the rest of the week. You know laundry and chores and all of that." Serena answered while she got up and leaned over to kiss Tasha. "But don't worry. I will see you at work tomorrow."

"Yes, I remember, there's apparently going to be some very long nights this next month…" Tasha smirked as Serena left the room to go home.

Abby's First Lesbian Experience With The Pizza Delivery Girl

By Jerry Forrest

Abby was a college student, living with her sorority sisters at a major land-grant university. She was a straight-A student throughout her entire school career, and was only a year away from graduating magna cum laude. She was planning on advancing to law school, hoping to become a big-city lawyer.

However, Abby was also very shy and insecure. She had a hard time meeting guys on campus. She didn't care for the nerds, and the jocks wanted nothing to do with her. The fraternity brothers knew her too well from all the joint work the various Greek houses did around the community, and was thus stuck in the "friend zone" with them.

One day, Abby and her sorority sisters were hungry and had no food at the sorority house. The sisters wanted Chinese, but Abby just wanted pizza. The sisters decide to go out and get some Chinese, while Abby decides to go ahead and order pizza for herself. Abby then calls the local pizza shop near campus.

"Hello, Guiseppe's Pizzeria. How may I help you today?" said a young man on the other end of the phone.

"Hi, what do you have on special today?" asks Abby.

"Well," said the gentlemen, "we are offering two 12-cut pizzas with up to three toppings for only $20."

Abby sounds impressed but, knowing she was eating by herself, knows that she doesn't need that much food. "OK, but it's just me eating. Do you have anything for one person?"

"Well ma'am, it would be a better deal just to get the 2-for-$20," replied the gentlemen. "If you want to, you can save the pizza for later, unless you plan to have company for later."

"Well, my sorority sisters went out to have Chinese and I'm home alone. Granted, Chinese isn't that filling and they may be hungry later. But, I don't want to take that chance."

The gentlemen pauses, knowing he has a tough sell. "Ma'am, one of my coworkers is actually about to get off. They haven't eaten all day. If you want to order two pizza's, I can have them deliver the pizza's to your house and they would be done for the day after that. If you have a credit card, you can pay for it over the phone and you don't have to worry about paying the delivery person."

"Well," says Abby, who at this point starts to perk up a bit. "I could use the company. I don't know how long my sisters will be gone. OK, get me the 2-for-$20. Both with pepperoni and extra cheese."

"Sounds good," says the gentleman. "The total after tax will be $21.20. Your order will be ready in about a half hour. Did you want to pay over the phone with your credit card?"

"Sure," says Abby, who then proceeds to give her credit card information over the phone. "I can't wait to have a companion for some pizza tonight!"

"Alright ma'am, we'll have your order ready in no time," responds the gentleman before hanging up.

Abby was excited for someone to be coming over. Although not unattractive in any way, she had more of a "girl next door" look than her sisters. She had long brown hair, wore glasses, and a typical hourglass figure you see on a woman. Her breast size was a C-cup, which on her 5'10" frame fit her pretty well. Her tall height was part of her problem attracting guys, as she was taller than many guys she knew on campus and were insecure of dating a woman who was taller than they were.

An hour has passed and the pizza hadn't arrived yet. Abby's roommate Ashley calls and tells her that the sisters decided to go bar hopping after eating dinner and wouldn't be home until late. Abby is about to call the pizza shop and wonder where her food is until she hears a knock at the door.

"Oh boy, my pizza is here. And so is my date!"

Abby opens the door to see the delivery person with her pizza. Much to her surprise, the delivery person is a woman.

"Hi Abby," says the delivery woman. "Sorry I'm late, I had to help the shop make some pizzas. We had the basketball team from the college come in and order ten pizzas. The pizza shop refunded your credit card due to the delay."

"Yeah, I was wondering why my pizza was taking so long," says Abby. "So I take it you're my dinner buddy?"

"Yep," says the delivery woman. "My name is Julie. I'm also a fellow student on campus. So glad to be off work."

"I was expecting a guy to come over," says Abby. "But, I guess I'll take another female companion instead. Come on in Julie."

Julie comes in the house and hangs her coat up on the door. The two girls start eating pizza and talk about their college experience. Abby tells Julie about wanting to go to law school, while Julie mentions she is in the nursing program. They then talk about their sexual exploits.

"I have a hard time meeting guys on campus," says Abby. "I'm not interested in nerds, the jocks want nothing to do with me, the frat boys see me as a sister, and most other guys are intimidated by my height."

"Hmmm…" responds Julie. "Have you ever thought about seeing what sex is like with a woman?"

"Well…I've never given it much thought. I do think some of today's actresses in Hollywood are attractive."

Julie brightens up when Abby says this. "Sounds like you're a little…bi-curious?"

Abby pauses for a second, then responds "I guess so."

"Great! Let me go out to my car. I'll be right back."

A few minutes later, Julie comes back in and carries a bag into the sorority house. She bends over and sits the bag on the floor, accidentally revealing a whale tail.

"You have a thong on?" asks Abby. "I've always thought those were uncomfortable."

"After a while you get used to it," says Julie, who then proceeds to take off her pants and shoes. "Did you want to start getting undressed?"

Abby looks confused at first, but decides to remove her shirt and pants to reveal her lingerie. Julie then removes her shirt and is also down to her lingerie. Julie is a little shorter than Abby at about 5'5", but has several tattoos covering her body. The rest of her proportions are similar to Abby. Julie then crawls up to Abby.

"So did you want to start making out then?"

Abby didn't hesitate, as she never got that much attention from a guy. "Sure!"

The two then start making out. Julie slowly removes her bra to reveal her breasts, which have nipple piercings. Abby does the same, but unlike Julie has no piercings. They both start to lay on the floor and eventually remove their panties as well. Julie crawls down Abby's chest and starts giving Abby oral sex.

"Wow…" says Abby, "I…uhh…haven't been there in a…uhhh…LONG time."

Julie stops for a second and says "Just shut up and let me eat your pussy."

Julie proceeds to give Abby oral sex for 20 minutes. Afterwards, Julie offers Abby to do the same to her, which she complies. Abby notices that Julie has a piercing on her clitorus.

"You have a piercing there?"

"Yes," says Julie. "It stimulates me faster. Now please eat me!"

Abby proceeds to give Julie oral sex for almost a half hour. Julie then goes to her bag and grabs a vibrator with a dildo attached. She proceeds to put the vibrator inside Abby's vagina and turns it on, while sucking on Abby's breasts.

"Oh…Ohh….OHHHHH! YES! YES! YES!" Abby was about to have an orgasm. "Fuck me some more bitch!"

Once finished, Julie then asks Abby to stick the vibrator inside her.

"Now I want you to do the same," says Julie. "But I want you to stick this inside of me anally."

"Isn't that going to hurt? I've had anal sex from a guy in the past and found it rather unpleasant."

"Trust me, I love anal sex. Just give it to me!"

Abby then proceeds to stick the running vibrator inside Julie's anus and crawls under her and sucks on her breasts. Julie nearly reaches full orgasm when they stop. The two take a quick break while Julie puts the vibrator back into her bag.

"So…" says a panting Julie, "You said anal was unpleasant, eh?"

"Yeah," responds Abby. "I consider it to be an exit only."

"Well, have you ever had…a shocker?"

66

"No, but I've heard of it."

"Did you want me to give you a shocker?"

Abby shows a look of concern, knowing her unpleasant past with anal sex. "Ummm...I would rather not."

"You know, you can reach full orgasm with a shocker."

Abby, knowing that she hasn't had a full orgasm in a long time and was due to be pleasured, decided to comply.

"Yes, I'll do it."

Julie then takes her left hand and sticks her index and middle finger into Abby's vagina and her pinky into Abby's anus. The two then start to make out while Julie is giving Abby the shocker. Abby then goes into a panic mode.

"OH YES! YES! YES!" Abby was pleasantly surprised. "IT'S COMING!"

Abby had reached full orgasm.

"Now," says Julie, "Do the same for me!"

Abby reciprocates Julie's request and also reaches full orgasm.

The two then lay on the floor cuddling together. They continue to kiss until Abby decides to speak.

"You know Julie," says Abby. "I was expecting a guy to come to the house to deliver that pizza. I was pleasantly wrong. And you guessed right that I was bi-curious."

"I kind-of figured," comments Julie.

"I want to thank you for the night we had tonight. I haven't had a night like this in a long time. And just so you know, I don't think I'm bi-curious anymore. I think I'm a full-blown lesbian."

Julie smiles at the remark. "I'm glad you feel this way. Do you think I can use your bathroom to shower real quick?"

"Sure. It's just upstairs, first door on your left."

Julie goes upstairs and showers. She comes back down and puts her clothes back on. Abby, who is still naked, hugs her for the wonderful night the two had and exchange phone numbers. They wish each other a good night, and Julie leaves with her bag in tow.

Not even five minutes after Julie leaves, Abby's sorority sisters come home. Still without clothes, they question what Abby had been doing all along.

"Abby," says her roommate Ashley. "Why are you naked?"

Knowing that they wouldn't believe her if she told them she just had the best sex of her life, Abby decides to make up a story. "Well...I like to walk around naked when I'm home alone. And now that you are here, I'm comfortable doing it when you are home."

Ashley looked dumbfounded. "I'd rather you'd have your clothes on when around us, but to each their own. Let's head up to our room."

The rest of the sorority sisters stay in the living room while Abby and Ashley head to their room, with Abby's clothes in a basket. Once in the room, Ashley then asks what happened when they were gone.

"Okay, what really happened? I know you're self-conscious about being naked in front of us. Did you just sleep with the pizza guy or something?"

Abby, who covers herself up with a blanket from her bed at this point, smiles and tells Ashley the truth.

"Well, kinda. I had sex with the pizza girl."

"Huh?" Ashley looked dumbfounded at this point.

"And it was the best sex I ever had! Shockers, vibrators, you name it!"

Ashley, knowing she's had her own sex escapades in the past, shrugs it off. "Well I'm glad you had a good evening. Had to be more eventful than our night eating Chinese and being around a bunch of obnoxious basketball players. Tomorrow is Sunday, we have a lot of studying to do for our midterms. Have a good night."

Abby goes to sleep knowing she had a good night. She never hears back from Julie, but she does go on to graduate from college magna cum laude, and goes on to law school where she passes the bar exam with flying colors and opens her own law firm. She indeed decides to date exclusively women from this point. To this day, she considers that one faithful night with a pizza woman helping her figure out who she really is.

Taylor's First Lesbian Experience: Taylor Can't Resist Emily and Emily Can't Resist That Juicy Pussy

By Alexia Engles

Taylor's lips were pink and her cheeks were flushed. Her breath came in shallow, short bursts. Her nipples were tiny gumdrops being tickled by Emily's tongue as it slid over them in circles. Her head tilted back and her long fingers slid through Emily's hair, tightening around the strands and pulling on them in an urgent plea. Taylor had never been with another girl before but she was finding it to be more of a turn-on than she'd ever felt with a guy. Was it because it was forbidden? Or was it because she'd known for months that Emily had wanted to show her the ropes and it gave her some satisfaction to finally allow Emily to do so?

"I want you to taste me," Taylor begged as moisture quickly soaked between her legs. If Emily could tease Taylor's nipples with such amazing precision, Taylor couldn't imagine what she could do with her clit.

Emily slowly straightened up and was level with Taylor. She had a mischievous smirk playing across her lips and a glimmering in her eyes. Suddenly without warning, Emily shoved Taylor backwards. She flailed her long, slender arms and fell back against the mattress. Before Taylor had time to process, Emily crawled over her.

"I'll taste you if you behave." That voice, strong and sultry, made Taylor squirm as her tingling skin became that much more desperate for contact. Emily let go of Taylor's forearms only to let her fingertips glide over Taylor's tingling breasts, then slowly down her midriff, and finally, after what felt like an eternity, those fingers slipped between Taylor's legs.

The moment Emily's fingers moved over Taylor's puffy lips, Taylor's back arched off of the bed and an involuntary moan escaped her throat. "Please, oh god Please!" She begged as the inner muscles of her pussy were already tightening with physical anticipation. She needed to be touched and it needed to be NOW. Emily waited a few agonizing moments before responding to Taylor's plea and finally letting her pointer finger slip between Taylor's pussy and tease her inner folds. Taylor arched again and her long-legs fell to the side, giving Emily easier access to her juicy center. Emily teased with her finger more, slipping it up to Taylor's swollen clit and running over it a few times forcing involuntary spasms to tear through Taylor's body. Her lips tickled at Taylor's sensitive neck as her finger slipped back into her wet, pink pussy. The tip of Emily's tongue teased under Taylor's right ear, and then Emily travelled downward. Her tongue teased Taylor's hard nipples once again.

72

Emily continued kissing a trail down Taylor's tummy as her hands slid over her legs. Taylor closed her eyes as Emily's warm breath fell over Taylor's throbbing pussy lips.

Finally, the flat of Emily's tongue pulled slowly upward, lapping at Taylors lips for that first initial taste. Taylor's mouth opened wide in surprise as she moaned loudly, raising her legs and letting them rest over Emily's shoulders. "Holy shit," she muttered, unable to do anything for the moment but let her head fall back against the pillow. Emily was in charge and they both knew it.

Emily's tongue slipped between Taylor's folds and began to taste the thick, sweet moisture that had been gathering, lapping at her lips like a thirsty dog. Taylor thrashed, her heels pressing down against Emily's back as her fingers gripped the sheet on either side of her. Emily teased Taylor's pussy with the tip of her tongue, circling it around her clit in a far more expert fashion than any guy had ever done to her before. The physical reaction was instantaneous. Electric shots rushed up Taylor's spine, making her entire body spasm. Her fingers left their grip on the sheet and returned to Emily's hair, tugging on it with such demand as Taylor spread her legs even wider. Emily moved her own fingers to spread Taylor's lips, exposing the pink wetness of her labia, only moving back up to Taylor's clit when she stopped shaking. "Oh my god. Baby, you're so good," Taylor encouraged and pleaded at the same time. How had she resisted this for so long? She'd crave this all the time now, every day, every night, whenever Emily wanted. She'd be Emily's fucking slave if Emily would be hers.

Emily's fingers moved to Taylor's legs, curling around them and digging into them. Taylor knew she'd have marks on her thighs later on and she didn't care in the least. Emily's tongue circled around her clit some more and then slid down to her pussy, slipping in and licking at her inner walls. She knew just where to lick, just how much pressure to lick with, and just when to stop mere moments before Taylor burst into orgasm. Emily was the ultimate tease. "Jesus Christ just let me CUM," Taylor panted, beating her heels down on Emily's back like a temper tantrum. Emily let out an almost inaudible chuckle and finally slid her tongue as far into Taylor's pussy as she could, while moving her thumb over her clit. Taylor closed her eyes as her back arched off the bed again. Her fingers yanked Emily's hair like she was tugging back reigns on a runaway horse. Finally that ball of electricity at the base of her spine exploded between her legs. She came hard and fast. Moisture squirt out of her pussy and soaked Emily's face like a fire hose. She screamed, completely letting go and basked in the fireworks that were rushing from inside her body to every single nerve ending on the surface of her skin. She shook and convulsed, her vaginal muscles spasmed, and her heartbeat raced.

Taylor barely noticed Emily move upward over her until she felt Emily's lips upon her own, letting her taste the fruits of Emily's labor. The sweet cum that soaked Emily's face soaked the bed sheet beneath them. Taylor had never tasted herself before, but she tasted good. She kissed Emily back slowly, letting the tip of her tongue move over Emily's lips. Taylor's body let out one final shudder and fell back helplessly against the mattress. For a few moments she simply laid there and focused on her breathing, noticing how quickly her chest was rising and falling, and how tingly the surface of her skin still was. She slowly turned to gaze upon Emily with hungry but satisfied blue eyes. "I'll do anything you want Master," she whispered to Emily.

Knowing she had won full control over Taylor's pussy, Emily devilishly asked "Anything?"

The Slave Lover: A Historical, Interracial, Lesbian Erotica

Krista Collar

As the Mistress of the estate, Sally Anne had a prestigious reputation to uphold. While her husband, Lord Rivers, was gone away to England on business; it was up to Mistress Sally to run the estate with a mighty fist. She had over thirty slaves on hand that worked the land. Rivers Estate produced tobacco, cotton and indigo that would be exported all over the world.

Mistress Sally was known to be ruthless, strict and dominant in her world. If it were not for her, Rivers Estate would not be as successful. It was the year 1822, and times were changing, adding even more pressure to her already blooming business venture.

As Sally Anne made her morning inspection around the fields, her sapphire eyes involuntarily settled on a certain slave that she had not noticed before. Her ebony skin glistened under the sunlight as she thoroughly concentrated on picking seeds from the cotton plants. Her pitch-black silky hair danced along with the warm southern wind. She was unlike any colored girl she had ever seen in her forty years of life. *Breathtaking.*

"Mae, tell me who that girl is over by the left cotton field." Sally ordered her trusted servant, Mae, to inform her of the mystery girl.

"Oh, yes Mistress Sally. That youngling over there is Natalia. She came here from Savannah, Georgia, two days ago. I thought you had been informed of her arrival."

Mistress Sally observed the hard working beauty. She admired the way her slender fingers worked gracefully around the cotton, the way her toned feminine features flexed and moved with poise. Natalia seemed awfully young compared to the Mistress, but as she watched her with much intent, a foreign feeling stirred near her womb that she had not felt since she first married her husband.

"What is her age?" Mistress Sally rubbed her chin lightly with her index finger, continuing to study her.

"Nineteen years, Mistress." *Oh my.* She thought to herself.

Natalia was not a child, but a young woman who blossomed beautifully into a rich flower that tempted her senses in a very sexual manner.

Sally Anne wanted to touch the tempting Apple standing just a few hundred feet away from her. The layered dress she was wearing suddenly felt tight and heavy. She squeezed her thighs together, pressing them as tightly as she could. A pool of wetness was now flowing like a raging river, ready to be released from the dam.

Just as she was about to walk away from her sinful temptations, Natalia peered over her shoulder, meeting the blazing eyes of her Mistress. The Ocean blue depths of her irises swirled with a burning desire of lust that took her breath away.

The Ebony girl's light brown eyes that seemed to be reading her soul captivated Sally Anne. There was no way she could stop her desires now. Natalia must be hers to taste, touch, smell and admire.

"Bring her to my manner right away. I must do my usual inspection." The Mistress quickly made up an excuse.

Natalia would be hers. Sally Anne had to be extremely precise and careful with what she was about to plunge herself into. If anyone found out, they would both be hanged in the town square as several spectators cheered for their cruel fate.

As Sally Anne impatiently waited in her husband's study, she heard a soft knock against the other side of the cherry oak wooden doors. The clicking of her heels, harshly hit the teak floors as she hurried to answer it. As soon as the door opened, a gush of wind brushed her skin and hit her with a soothing aroma of vanilla and an earthly smell.

Natalia.

There stood her young goddess along with the hefty Miss Mae. Sally Anne stepped aside, allowing the girl to enter, but quickly blocked the entrance once more when Miss Mae tried to come in as well. She dismissed her for an hour, telling her to finish her rounds.

"I'm sorry, Mistress. I apologize for upsetting you. Please don't whip me." A terror stricken Natalia pained Sally's heart. She never meant to frighten the poor girl.

Her voice soothed her ears with her faint, French accent. Natalia possessed a natural beauty that most women would fawn over. She definitely probably turned heads as she walked through a town or field. But Natalia belonged to her now, and a wave of jealousy washed through her at the thought of someone else touching her ebony beauty.

"No, Natalia. I want something from you."

Natalia raised a brow in a state of confusion, but parted her lips when she saw her Mistress charging toward her like a ravenous bull. Sally Anne stood tall over Natalia, wrapping her arms around her slim waist, and pulling their bodies together.

Mistress Sally's lips crashed harshly down onto Natalia's plump lips. *So soft*. Sally Anne lost herself as she lost herself in Natalia's sweet taste. She was like a delectable dessert that she never wanted to finish and have everyday for her own pleasure.

Natalia felt her arms wrapping around her Mistress' neck, pulling her even closer. She parted her mouth open when she felt her tongue dancing along her lower lip. Their tongues intertwined sensuously in an erotic dance of passion and possession. In that one euphoric kiss, Sally Anne was letting her know whom she belonged to, and Natalia gladly accepted her claim on her.

Ripping her blouse open with her bare hands, Sally Anne hated having to pry her lips away from Natalia. She groaned when she saw her large dark breasts popping out from the fabric that held them to her chest. Sally immediately lowered herself down and began sucking and tugging Natalia's dark nipple. Her hand kneaded and massaged her other breast that filled her hand perfectly.

Natalia tilted her head back and parted her lips, releasing a small moan. Her black hair fell from her shoulders and down the curvature of her back. Her nipples stiffened from the amazing feel of her Mistress' touch.

To Sally, Natalia was everything she wanted her to be. Beautiful, sexy, dedicated, and from what she could tell by her voice… intellectual. Her aura radiated a sophisticated energy that swept through Sally's cold exterior. She hadn't had a sexual encounter in over a year. Her husband never pleasured her, only pleasured himself in less than three minutes.

Just by hearing her moan, Sally had a small orgasm rupture throughout her center. It was intoxicating and addicting. She needed and craved more of Natalia. She pulled her onto the floor and laid her over the Persian rug. Her hair sprawled out around her like a lush crown, and her breasts rested peacefully as they called silently to Sally for her touch.

Sally placed herself over Natalia's petite form and connected their lips once more. Her hand travelled up her inner thigh, and soon she felt her fingers slip between her silky folds. Natalia moaned in delight as Sally created circular patterns around her clit in a repetitive motion. Her fingers were coated with a thick wetness. Sally brought her now wet hand to Natalia's lips and began tracing her finger around their soft outline.

"Taste yourself, love." Sally whispered seductively.

Natalia licked her tongue around her lips, tasting herself. Sally couldn't resist her own urges, as she flickered her tongue around Natalia, selfishly wanting her own sample of her tempting beauty. She inwardly smiled as she savored her taste of a sweet honey. Sally knew that she could never tire of Natalia, even if she tried.

"*Mistress,*" Natalia breathed out in pure elation.

Natalia wrapped her lean legs around her Mistress, grinding her cleft against the soft material of her dress. Sally arched her hips forward, meeting Natalia with each small thrust. She watched as she allowed the tempting beauty lost herself in a world of intense pleasure.

"That's it my darling. Come for your Mistress." She cooed to her.

With those simple words, Natalia was hit with a ravenous orgasm that coursed deep throughout her body. It rippled in a series of pleasurable waves that lasted for minutes. It was Natalia's very first orgasm, and she was hooked.

When she finally opened her eyes, she looked ahead of her to see her Mistress completely unclothed. She was stunning, and beautiful for an older woman. Her blonde curly locks, hung over her small perky breasts. Natalia felt an itch to run her hands all over her.

Sally Anne sat on the rug, wrapping her hands around her ankles and pulling Natalia to her. She pried her legs open forcefully with hungry eyes. Sally opened her legs as well, and scooted Natalia between her as their legs scissored together. Their wet pussies met and slid against each other, mixing their juices together.

When Natalia got the gist of it, they both began to rub themselves against each other in a synchronized motion. Sweat began to glisten over their heated bodies, and the smell of sex lingered heavily in the room. They pressed into each other even harder as the tingles and waves of euphoria began hitting them even harder than before.

"Oh, yeah! Mistress! It feels so good!" Natalia yelled out in ecstasy.

Sally Anne began breathing heavily, lifting her hips and rolling them in a circular motion, their bodies and souls becoming one in the process. She felt her womb tightening as a large orgasm was approaching fast and furiously.

Sally latched tightly onto Natalia's hips, and grinded against her a few more times before feeling her own release. The water from her dam finally began to release itself and it was magnificent. It was unlike anything she'd ever felt before.

The two women faced a series of aftershocks that travelled through their anatomies. The air was stuffy from their hitched breathing, and sweat covered them. Their apertures were soaked in each other's wetness.

They both leaned into one another and licked their pussies clean, tasting each other one final time.

Sally and Natalia knew that there would be more encounters between the two of them. Lord Rivers would be gone another three months, but she didn't want him. There was something about Natalia that brought Sally Anne to life. The fire that she thought had burned out in her soul was now igniting and blazing more than ever. She was addicted to this little slave girl, but to Sally she would be her lover.

A Six-Girl Lesbian Orgy with a Clit Pump and Strap On

By Alexia Engles

I woke up one morning and realized it's been 3 months since my divorce from Adam. Which also means, it's been at least 3 months that I hadn't had sex. I was never quite spontaneous when it came to sex anyway, which is why I think things went wrong in my marriage. Here I am, 29 years old and I have never given oral nor have I received it. All I ever done was lie on my back and waited for him to finish. Adam always made me feel the absolute worse when it came to our sex life and how boring it was.

One night, Adam called and said that he would be working late. I began to get very bored so I made my sister's favorite cake and decided to surprise her by bringing her a slice. I went into her home (I had a spare key), and heard some hot and very intense erotic sounds. "UHH OHHH FUCK ME!" I slightly giggled at the thought of my sister having sex. Although it was my sister having sex, I couldn't help but enjoy the sounds of her wetness. Curiosity drew me closer to the sounds. As I peeked into her bedroom, I watched as she hopped up and down on a very engorged man. It wasn't until she screamed, "OHHH ADAMM!" that I quietly left without interrupting them and cried uncontrollably on the way home. To this day I don't talk to Adam or my sister.

Sensing my depression, my best friends decided that we should go out for drinks and then go back to my house to spend the night. I'm living in a huge five bedroom home, so I figured it couldn't do any harm. As the evening approached, I began to get ready and realized after all the weight I've lost over the past three months, I must say I actually look great. I carefully removed the clothes I had on and began touching myself. Starting with my lips, I began to suck on my middle finger and gently moved it down to my nipples as they became erect. I have extremely huge boobs and therefore I am able to suck them. As I begin flickering my tongue on my nipples and gently nibbling on them, I felt a warm and sticky wetness run down my legs. I took my fingers and slowly began rubbing my clit. By this time it had become really swollen and sensitive to the touch. At that moment I knew I was gonna cum.

I took two fingers and inserted them into my vagina. I damn near exploded at that moment when I heard a knock on the door. "TRACEY ARE YOU IN THERE?" my friend Shelia yelled out while banging on my door.

"Yeah, just a minute," I replied.

I opened the door for her and she said, "Am I interrupting something?"

"No," I replied, "I was just getting ready to get in the shower." As she went upstairs and sat on my bed she rubbed her hand over a wet spot and said, "Eww, what is this?"

I said "I spilled something over there." I looked guilty as ever.

Knowing what I had done she asked, "No you didn't, you were masturbating weren't you?" After five minutes of trying to convince Shelia I wasn't masturbating, she cut me off and said, "It's okay. I do it every day. But hurry up, we have reservations with the other girls, and I don't want to be late."(Shelia hasn't been in a relationship in over a year).

I rushed into the shower and decided to pick up where I left off since I never got a chance to cum. I tried my best to be quiet but as soon as I approached my climax my moans and heavy breathing got louder. Shelia in the next room creeped into my bathroom, and grabs my butt. "Oww Shelia, what the fuck?"

Shelia laughed out loud and said, "Why are you so ashamed? It's natural. Here let me show you how to do it." At this point I was frustrated and curious to what she had to say. She instructed me to lie down on my back and use the shower head to aim it directly on my pussy. Even though I was uncomfortable with the situation I did as she said, and boy, am I glad I did. The pressure of the water hitting my clit was so intense; I began to moan louder than I ever had with any other man. I was caught up in the moment. I began to caress my breast, biting down on my lip. Shelia must have become aroused by watching me as she slowly undressed and got in the shower and began kissing me. Her tongue tasted so sweet as if she just finished eating a starburst. I felt that this was wrong, but I was enjoying it and it was too far to turn back now. Shelia got up quickly and said motioned to go in the room, so I agreed with a nod.

At this moment my heart was pounding. She pushed me on the bed and began sucking on my neck, then chest and stomach. As she got closer to my pussy, I felt all tingly inside. She kissed my inner thighs and sucked on them. Sometimes she gently bit them. Finally the moment that I have been waiting for: she took her wet tongue and slowly licked my clit. Her wet tongue drove me crazy and felt better than any dick I ever had in my life. She took her tongue and stuck it in and out of my pussy. I didn't know what to do with myself. Right at the moment I was about to cum, she stopped and places herself on top of me (as if she was a man). She took her clit and placed it on mine and began to grind. The grinding was so intense that one minute in I came. I could feel the juices from her pussy and that drove me insane. Soon after, she came also.

Thinking it was over, she stood over me and positioned herself to sit on my face. Even though I didn't have any experience, I immediately knew what to do. I licked and sucked her clit, but what drove me crazy was when she began riding my tongue as if it was a dick. She came inside my mouth, and I didn't mind at all. Realizing that we were an hour late, we jumped up and promised each other we would never tell what happened, as I have never been with a woman and neither has she. Dinner went great and now me and my five friends (Shelia, Debra, Ashley, Victoria, and Yasmine) were heading back to my place to watch movies and have more drinks.

The night had been going really well until I had way too many drinks and began thinking about Adam. I began to cry and my friends reassured me that things will get better and that I should lie down. About 45 minutes into my nap I felt a hand run in between my thighs and a hand over my mouth. The hand made its way to my pussy so I turned over expecting Shelia. However, it was Yasmine. She whispered into my ear, "Shelia told me what you two did earlier, and now I want my chance."

Even though Yasmine is my friend, I always felt that she would be the one to sleep with my ex-husband as she was really experienced with sex. I was angry at Shelia, but my anger quickly turned into excitement as Yasmine removed my clothing as well as hers. Unlike Shelia, Yasmine wasn't a tease and got straight to the point. She positioned herself so that we would be in a 69 position and to my surprise I noticed that Yasmine's clitoris was a little larger than normal, butt it didn't take away from her womanhood. I sucked the slightly larger clit as she began grinding on my face. She stopped suddenly (I was thinking we were caught), and said, "Wait here."

She came back with a weird looking device, so I asked, "What is that?"

"A clit pumper" she replied. "It makes your clitoris larger." As she began pumping her clit, I watched as it grew even larger than what it was. When she finished, she told me to lay back and spread my legs open. She placed her clit in my vagina and it drove me crazy. The sounds were beyond indescribable. In and out, in and out is all I could remember during that pleasurable time. Shelia must have told the other girls about our little fun we had earlier because all of the girls were coming in to join us. Three months ago I would have not agreed to this and would have been embarrassed if someone asked me to but tonight was a different story. Yasmine stopped before she could orgasm and gave everyone directions. She said to me, "Just lay there." The she told Ashley to sit on my face, Victoria to eat me while Debra eats her, and she will eat Debra while Shelia rams her from the back with a strap on, that way we could all enjoy. It seemed a bit confusing, but I was up for the challenge.

It was one big lesbian orgy fest and I was enjoying every minute of it. I even took my turn fucking the girls with the strap on. I really came out of my shell that night. The fun lasted a while until we all passed out from the multiple orgasms we each had. The next morning, none of us wanted to take ownership of what we did last night. We even blamed it on the alcohol. However, we all agreed that we would get together and have "drinks" at least a few times a week.

Early Morning Lesbian Delights: Oral and Scissoring to Start the Day

Alexia Engles

I slowly awake and open my eyes to see her still lying next to me, her large beautiful breasts with areola the size of perfect silver dollars and pink little nipples that are standing straight up. I reach down to gently caress my pussy for just a moment before pulling back the sheets and moving my head in between her long tight legs. No panties in the way, she sleeps without them. I begin to gently kiss the inside of her thighs moving all the way around kissing teasing her tight little pussy. Her body starts to twist trying to move her sweet little opening closer to my wandering tongue. I begin to suck on the wings that remind me of a stingray, slowly stretching them out staring up at her who though still writhing her hips closer to me lies with her eyes closed and is breathing softly, still sleeping.

I then begin to dart my tongue around her clit, sucking and tasting while it becomes larger in my mouth. Slipping my tongue slowly down her lips I find the honeypot so wet, so salty as I begin to gently tongue the juices like a cat drinking milk. She slowly opens her eyes and looks down at me with a dreamy smile on her face.

With one hand between my own legs gently massaging my clitoris I move my left hand up and quickly thrust my ring and middle finger up into her tight little hole. As she gasps with joy, I continue to thrust my fingers inside of her rhythmically while still sucking ferociously onto her clit.

Her thighs clench around my ears blocking out all the beautiful noises she made squealing with joy. Don't stop, her body tells me as I continue to suck and fuck long past my hand crying out in pain to stop. All of a sudden the thighs clench unbearable tight around my ears and as soon as I think my head is going to pop from all of the pressure the thighs relax and I can hear her breathing heavily with all of her wet juices flowing onto the sheets. I begin to gently lap up all of my reward as she continues to slowly move her clit up and down over my tongue.

Our eyes meet and she smiles. Suddenly she reaches down grabs a clump of hair from my head and pulls me up to her level to kiss her. My tongue slowly swirls around hers, still flavored. She giggles and throws me over onto my back and while pushing my hands into the mattress so they cannot be moved. She begins to nibble on each ear then licks her way down to my chest where she sucks on one nipple before moving to the pierced nipple with the little ring in it that she grabs with her teeth and gently pulls away from my body stretching my breast out.

As she continues to pull and suck on my breast her other hand reaches down between my legs to find my panties are completely soaked through. Upon discovering the wetness she let go of my arms to reach down and rip my panties off getting frustrated with getting them off and leaving them hanging on one foot before diving her face into my warm wet pussy. Her face immediately started moving back and forth with her tongue as I started thrusting my hips up and down. I could do nothing but close my eyes and appreciate the thickness of her perfect tongue as it explored my entire pussy before jamming several fingers inside of me. She began to lift me with her hand that was inside of me while continuing to suck on my clitoris.

As I moved my fingers into her hair and pushed her head deeper into my pussy she thrust me harder and harder until all of the warmth and pleasure coming from between my legs exploded throughout my entire body. She continued to gently suck and lick the lips and clit as I moaned with pleasure for several minutes. She then lifted her body next to mine began kissing me while wrapping her legs around my hips and grinding her still juicy pussy onto the moist mound between my legs. I reach up and grab onto her perfect love handles and gently digging my nails into the flesh on her hips I pull her into me smashing our bodies together. She leans completely on top of me while riding me and has one hand firmly pulling a fistful of hair and the other roughly scratching up and down my back.

Together we thrust and ride each other with little bites into one another's flesh until we each freeze with immense pressure mounting between our bodies with out nails digging even further into one another's skin and a strained moan of pleasure escaped from her lips as she bit her bottom lip with her top teeth. Now our sweaty bodies slide together as we collapse into one another and gently drift back off into sleep.

Eating Pussy and Soaking Sheets: A Lesbian Erotica

By Alexia Engles

There was a drop of sweat trailing down her breast, lighting up her nerves like the fucking Fourth of July. Frankie had told her to keep her hands behind her back so she couldn't wipe the sweat away, couldn't drag her nails over her nipples or drag her breast up to her own mouth so she could at least fucking suck--

"Lisa." Frankie was the kind of girl Lisa had dreamed of getting fucked by, had never thought would give her the time of day. Now Frankie was ducked under Lisa's bent head, quirking an eyebrow, a smug little smile on her face. "Lisa," she said again, "if you don't bend over for me you're going to regret it."

Lisa was wet, soaking, the sheet was already soaking under her, her ankles slick from where she was sitting on them. "My hands," Lisa said, "I can't, I want to, how," the words jumbling out, she tried to say them so fast.

"The headboard," Frankie said. She put her hand at the back of Lisa's neck, guiding her down until her forehead rested on the headboard, the rest of her bent over with her hands behind her back. Lisa could feel cool air touching the wet heat of her pussy, spread open and dripping with the position.

And then Frankie crawled down the bed and pressed her face against Lisa's snatch, inhaling deeply before licking at the juices like she was trying to drink Lisa dry. Every press of Frankie's tongue against the side of Lisa's clit shot another bolt of lightning through Lisa, driving her against forward against the headboard, backward into Frankie's face, a rhythm that wasn't what she wanted.

Fuck it, Lisa thought, and used both hands to push herself away from the headboard and all the way back onto Frankie's face.

"My game now," Lisa said, and settled herself over Frankie's mouth. "But definitely keep going." Frankie's eyes widened, and then glazed a little at the thought of what Lisa was offering.

This time when Frankie dove in, Lisa could felt Frankie's hands on her thighs, grabbing her cheeks and spreading her wider. This time Lisa could see what Frankie was doing, could watch as Frankie closed her eyes and licked as delicate as a cat, her mouth and lips and face, God, just her face covered in Lisa's cream.

Drops of sweat landed on Frankie's face, flung from Lisa's swinging breasts, and fuck, she could touch those now, Lisa raked her nails over her nipples, felt the sharp spikes of pain and pleasure arrow straight down to her cunt. And--shit, she'd wanted to, why the fuck not--she lifted her left breast and got the nipple into her mouth, sucked it hard enough to bruise and hit that pinpoint electric nerve that always brought her close to edge.

"Fuck fuck fuck," Frankie chanted against her cunt as she stared up at Lisa. Frantically she started sucking up against Lisa's clit, her hand shifting from Lisa's thigh to the folds of her pussy. Frankie's thumb rubbed against the hood while one, two, three, the rest of her fingers slid inside her, curving and pressing and twisting exactly right, as if Frankie fucked her every night, as if Frankie had been the only one to fuck her, would be the only one to fuck her from now on, because no one could ever do it so well again.

When Lisa was wet, she soaked through sheets. When Lisa came, she ejaculated like a fucking firehose. Come sprayed across Frankie's face, thin liquid that coated Frankie's mouth and eyes, her hair, dripping down until it pooled in the creases under her head. Lisa knew she was supposed to feel embarrassed about it, maybe ashamed.

She wanted to fuck Frankie into the mattress.

Frankie probably wasn't feeling that was about it, though. Gingerly, Lisa lifted herself off and sat loosely next to Frankie, trying to ignore the hazy urge to sleep. She cleared her throat. "I'm, uh, sorry about--"

Frankie shook her head, her own glazed expression clearing a little. With one hand she carefully swiped at her face, collecting a generous coating of Lisa's lubricant. And then she just as carefully lifted her knee and spread the thick, sweet smelling juice across and into her own pussy.

"Lisa, you pretty, pretty girl," Frankie said, smiling a very different smile than her smug one, "get over here. My game now."

Scissoring a Stranger at the Beach: A Lesbian Erotic Tale with Oral Sex

By Hannah Butler

It happened by accident. Marissa had only come to the beach that day to try and relax. She wasn't looking for her at all. It was the hour just before sun set, right when the sun starts to blur against the sky and paint a fantastic array of colors reflecting them into a seemingly endless body of water. It felt natural to just fall asleep like right there, drifting off into a dream with a book resting against her chest as she committed my body to slumber. It was a well-deserved break after the tiresome week she'd suffered through at work.

She must have been asleep for all of an hour when she heard a voice softly calling out to her.

"Excuse me" Marissa heard a female voice saying, but they must have been talking to someone else, there were a few other people there and she'd been sitting by herself.

"Excuse me" she heard again, this time just a little louder.

Blinking her eyes, Marissa squinted just enough to see the thin waving outline of a towel she'd wrapped herself in. It was now in another woman's hands. Briefly, she dismissed the woman with a wave of her hand and tried to fall back asleep. But, a sudden recollection wouldn't allow her the relaxation she desired. Another woman had seen her without her towel. Her eyes shot open at the realization. A towel she needed because she'd been so busy with work she'd skipped her monthly bikini wax. Her eyes peered down toward her bikini line. Yep, it still looked like a hairy untamed forest peeking out of her bottoms. DAMN IT she cursed to herself. Looking up again she saw that the other woman was still standing in front of her. DAMN IT she cursed again.

"Mind if I sit here?" The other woman asked while pointing at an unoccupied beach chair next to Marissa.

She'd been expecting something else, for the other woman to call her out, to say something about the unruly mess of tangled hair that Marissa had unintentionally exposed. Maybe she hadn't noticed after all. "Good" Marissa thought as she wrapped the towel back around herself.

"Sure"

With that she closed her eyes again determined to finally get some rest. She was just nodding off when she felt a light tap on her shoulder. It was the other woman again. Marissa was beginning to feel a slight twinge of irritation. But she figured she may as well try to be nice, she'd already gone through the trouble of returning her towel.

"Sorry, I just was wondering if you're not reading that book…"

Without hearing anything else Marissa quickly handed it over. She felt her towel slip just slightly as she did so, but she paid no attention to it and was quickly back to sleep.

It couldn't have been that long, ten or fifteen minutes at the most before Marissa felt stirred again by the sound of the other woman, but she was still groggy and couldn't make out what was being said. Her eyes blinked open and she turned to her left just far enough to catch sight of what had been going on. The blonde stranger next to Marissa had been caught with her hands inside her own bikini bottoms desperately trying to cum.

"What the hell!" Marissa screeched. But the stranger seemed undeterred and continued pleasuring herself feverishly, her moans becoming louder and more frequent.

Their eyes met and it seemed, with a desperate, hungry, wonton look, the stranger was begging Marissa to drop the towel completely.

"I'm just going to go!" Marissa protested. But, in her haste to get up she'd completely forgotten about the towel and it fell to the ground around her. She turned to leave, but the blond had taken hold of her arm now and she felt stuck there watching with increased excitement as this stranger finger-fucked her pussy while staring at Marissa's fluffy mound.

At least no one could see them she tried to assure herself. As the wetness she felt between her thighs became too hard to ignore. She didn't know what had come over her. But, she figured if she couldn't fall asleep, there were a few other ways to relax she could think of. She lowered her bottoms just enough to reveal the unkempt jungle of course red hair hiding underneath. The blond took hold of Marissa's bottoms and snuck her hand inside. She started by petting, but soon she was running her fingers through the mess of curly red pubs as she continued working her clit. Marissa felt the other woman's fingers dancing against the sensitive skin of her clit as she continued to swirl them around the plentiful mess of pub hairs.

Taking her hand away from her own pussy, the blond offered them up to Marissa's waiting and eager mouth. The taste of the other woman's pussy in her mouth was like a pleasure bomb exploding in her mouth. She needed more. Stepping over to the front of the other woman's chair Marissa knelt down so that her mouth met perfectly with the blonde's swollen crotch. She licked at the fabric of her bikini bottoms and felt the outline of a thick tuft of hair concealing the stranger's pulsating walls.

"I'm going to suck your furry clit until you cum" Marissa explained and the blonde responded by arching her back so that her pelvis lifted upward toward Marissa's mouth.

She licked at it thirstily before stripping the other woman of her bottoms, revealing a wide landing strip of sweaty blond curls. Arousal grew inside Marissa as she continued sucking and licking blindly, encouraged by the other woman's ravenous moaning. Neither of them seemed at all concerned about the audience they'd attracted, it only excited them more. Soon Marissa felt the blonde's fingers slipping inside her working in and out of her walls.

She kept her head buried in her partner's lap swallowing every secretion as they came to her. The folds grew thicker inside her mouth and she could tell the blonde was near climax. She kept at it, increasing her pace until the blonde begged her for mecy.

"I need your fingers inside me please."

Marissa complied. Keeping her mouth fixed on the blonde's bushy muff she added two fingers, thrusting them in and out as she continued to lick at the other woman's throbbing clit. It didn't take long before she felt the other woman's body relax and her toes curl into the sand as the blonde's pussy squirted a messy stream of cum inside of Marissa's mouth and all over her face.

Crawling onto the reclining beach chair so that her body rested on top of the blonde's, Marissa slipped her bikini bottoms to the side exposing her fat and hairy pussy. She wrapped their legs around each other and began rubbing her pussy against the other woman's already exposed clit. She grabbed tightly onto the other woman, kissing her passionately as her walls trembled. The blonde swiveled her hips and hitched back and forth, increasing the heat of their contact. When she wasn't expecting it the other woman sucked down on Marissa's neck and then bit just hard enough to send Marissa's nerves over the edge. Her legs went limp as she came, her body relaxed and fell on top of the blonde. They stayed like that for a while, their pussies meshed up in each other a tangled mess of intermingled cum swirled around red and blonde curls. Marissa rested her head against the other woman's bountiful heaving bosom and drifted off one last time.

When she woke again she found the fading sun had disappeared and she was now greeted by the bright glow of the moon. Her lover's nude body still resting underneath her, Marissa gathered her things, gave the other woman one last kiss on the cheek and left to go back home. She didn't think much of her crazy night at the beach for the rest of the weekend. She was grateful to the stranger, whoever she'd been for helping her unwind, but they hadn't even exchanged names. There wasn't much for Marissa to go on. She told herself she just had to not think about it.

So, by the time Monday rolled around she'd successfully shoved it to the back of her mind. She had work to do, and lots of it. There were three mountain sized stacks of client files waiting for her when she got into the office and as soon as she sat down to go through them, her phone started ringing incessantly. Someone from legal was calling in to her office repeatedly; she'd ignored it in an effort to focus on the client files. But, after the fifth call she relented and was immediately startled by the voice on the other end of the phone.

"If you have a minute there are some things I'd like to go over with you."

Marissa felt nervous, she didn't want to ask. But, she agreed to meet and quickly made her way to the third floor to an office with a name plate that read Alana Frost. Sure enough, it was the woman from the beach. Marissa stepped inside the office shutting the door behind her.

Grabbing a book off of her desk Alana offered it to Marissa "I thought you might want this back"

She couldn't take her eyes off of Marissa she was desperate to get her hands on the other woman's fire-red crotch again.

"You said there was something you wanted me to go over?" Marissa wondered aloud.

Walking over to the door Alana checked to make sure it was locked. She then dropped her skirt and walked over to where Marissa had been standing.

"How about you go over my clit with your tongue" she whispered.

Marissa thought again about how good Alana's pussy had tasted that night at the beach, she was salivating at the thought of having it again. She knew one thing for sure, work was starting to look a whole lot less stressful now.

She Makes Her Pet Slut Bark: A Lesbian, Slave and Master, Fisting Erotic Story

By Hannah Butler

Trica sat quietly on the floor, her eyes shut and her breath coming in little gasps. The clock, hanging high on the opposite wall of her spartan room, ticked away toward 6, toward her Mistress. A deep blush flushed across Trica's cheeks. She couldn't wait.

As her breathing changed from staccato gasps to a prolonged moan, Trica slipped two fingers inside her cunt and began to thrust. With skill honed by long hours of practice, and lust heightened by the combination of loneliness and transgression, Trica built the foundations of a towering orgasm with practiced strokes. Gradually probing deeper with her delicate fingers-one knuckle, now to, wait, wait for the third-she began working herself into a lather. With her pussy swollen and beginning already to spasm under her teasing ministrations, Tricia decided to drop the capstone onto her sexual colossus. Her thumb came down, gentle but firm, pressing her clit and running in maddening circles.

The pressure in her pelvis building to unbearable levels, Tricia tilted her head and arched her back as if to leave her body behind altogether. The joyful spasms of her tormented cunt reached an alarming pace as she played in the folds of her flesh. As Trica sensed her orgasm fast approaching she flung her legs wide, spreadeagled toward the door of her little room. If only she could have waited... If only mistress could come through the door and see her like this. And then the orgasm took her and left her howling, and writing on the ground, all plans suddenly dispelled, until she collapsed at last like a marionette with its strings cut.

Trica's eyes finally snapped open again and snapped to the clock. 6:05.

Shit Shit Shit!

Trica sprang to her unsteady feet and lurched toward the door. There was no time for hiding the evidence of her clandestine fun now, and no time to dread. Mistress was home and she, Trica, was late!

As Trica pelted down the long hallway from her small quarters off the master-bedroom she was lost to thought.

What will mistress think of me? Why couldn't I wait? Stupid Trica! Another fifteen minutes and I could have just asked her. Another fifteen minutes and I might not have needed to... Mistress was, after all, a sexual creature. Stupid, stupid Trica!

As she reached the narrow servant's stairs to the kitchen Trica's thoughts took and abrupt turn.

What will mistress do to me?

Trica could see her lover's car parked neatly in the driveway, where it always went. She could smell her Mistress' enchanting perfume already-she must have reapplied as soon as she'd come home. Maybe she won't be angry. She's so understanding after all, and she certainly doesn't mind when I cum with her. Maybe she will mind...

Trica was plunging down the stairs two at a time now.

...maybe she'll decide to show me the error of my ways.

Trica came to a breathless halt at the doorway of the kitchen. Her mistress was there, sitting with her back to the door and the day's paper open in front of her. Trica took a breath, composing herself as best she could, and took a step into the doorway.

"Good evening mistress, I'm so glad to see you."

Thinking, waiting for a reply, Trica realized she really was glad. Glad to see her lover, her mistress, home again, even if it might mean an evening of trouble for her. Trica's thoughts wandered back to the present and she found her mistress looking her up and down with a wry smile.

"So I see." Mistress purred, her eyes fixed on the floor between Trica's legs.

To her horror, Trica was suddenly aware of the heat between her hips and the wet little plop as beads of sweet and her own cum fell to the floor between her feet. Trica blushed scarlet for the second time that evening and fixed her Mistress with wide frightened eyes.

"I'm sorry, so sorry," she breathed hoarsely.

Her Mistress chuckled, studying her.

"For the floor, pet?"

"No..."

"No," Mistress agreed. "I thought not."

A smile, Trica saw, twitched in the corners of Mistress' mouth. Hopeful, she tilted her head in a silent question. With a sigh somewhere between bemused and long-suffering Mistress let her smile brighten all over her face as she held Trica's gaze.

"Come here and tell me what the matter is," Mistress instructed, patting her knee to indicate the

seat she had in mind.

Tricia stared shame-faced, but strangely excited, at the patch of tile between her feet and began to speak haltingly. "Well, Mistress-and I really did try not to-I couldn't manage the whole day with you gone. I'm not used to being apart from you yet, and you work for so long. I know it really is my own fault. I should have kept my hands out of my cunt, but I just couldn't do it."

Trica, breathless, brought her recriminations to an unceremonious halt and began to shiver slightly, anticipating a firm chastisement. To her shock, Mistress laughed softly in her ear. "I knew you were a slutty little thing, pet, but I had no idea how silly."

"What?" replied Trica, peering over her shoulder in disbelief.

Mistress suppressed her renewed laughter with great difficulty to purr again into the ear of her confused lover.

"I never said anything about not touching yourself while I was gone, Trica dear. I'm quite flattered. Really!" she insisted, seeing the crestfallen look on Trica's face. "But I'd rather my girl had fun while I was gone. Besides," she added with a casual wiggle of her knee against Trica's crotch, "I can see you haven't spoiled your appetite."

Trica's already formidable blush deepened as she squeaked, "No mistress."

With that, Trica found herself pushed unceremoniously onto the tile of the kitchen floor. Mistress began adjusting her position. She whistled, half absent minded and half leering, as she pulled Trica's hips up and pushed her head down. The cold tiles pressed against Trica's breasts and cheek, the slight discomfort and unceremonious presentation only enhancing the novice submissive's humiliation and arousal.

Mistress, at last satisfied with her lover's posture, reached to fondle her pet's exposed labia. At the sharp intake of Trica's breath she bent down to plant a kiss in whisper silkily into an ear. "You're determined to be 'naughty,' it only seems fair to treat you like it. I'm going to take you like a bitch in heat."

Trica didn't trust herself to answer. She gave the only response she could muster by inching her legs wider. Trica's Mstress leaned in with a predatory smile, slamming her pet's face into the tile with one hand and continuing to tease Trica's cunt with the other. Mistress' fingers danced tantalizingly along Trica's slit. They tickled and teased, probed delicately but refused to enter.

Trica, already beside herself with need, began to rock back on to her Mistress' hand. Mistress laughed at Trica's desperation, pushing her pet's head more firmly against the kitchen tile, but finally relented. The talented fingers of Mistress' right hand slipped between Trica's slick lips to thrust long, smooth, and hard into her sopping cunt. All the response Trica could muster, sprawled indecorously with her sensitive anatomy exposed to predatory attentions and brisk air alike, were incoherent pleas.

Suddenly, Mistress spat. A thick strand of saliva landed squarely on Trica's pussy and dripped with delicious degradation toward the floor. Trica, fast approaching the limit of her bodily control felt her cunt spasm around Mistress' fingers. The first wave of her orgasm was going to crash and there was nothing she could do but welcome it.

A sharp slap across the ass jerked Trica back from her oncoming climax even while fast, thrusting fingers drove it onward faster.

"Not yet." Mistress growled through tight lips. "Beg for it."

Trica, struggling against the tide of her desire, could only mewl into the floor in reply. Another sharp slap landed on her ass. Then another and another. The blows piled up on Trica's soft flesh. Each smack now landed with enough force to send juice from her overstimulated pussy flying through the air in little droplets. Still, all Trica could do was twitch and gibber with tears streaming down her cheeks and a whole fist now burred in her cunt.

"Bark then if you won't beg." Mistress hissed into Trica's ear. "Bark, Bitch. Bark, Pet."

Trica moaned into the floor. It hurt unbearably now to resist the orgasm threatening to overwhelm her. It was all she could do not to give in. Trica moaned again and whimpered. With enormous effort, she seized control of her tongue and throat again.

Bark

Bark Bark

And then it was over. Wave after wave of orgasm wracked Trica's body. Her cunt clenched and spasmed around Mistress' hand. The world went dark as she finally squeezed her eyes shut and gave in to a world of pure sensation.

Minutes later, Trica peeled her eyes open to find her Mistress kneeling over her, grinning. The powerful woman silhouetted against the kitchen light bent down and planted a mercifully tender kiss on Trica's quivering lips.

"My pet slut."

Can't Get Enough Pussy: An Erotic Lesbian Story

By Hannah Butler

It was the summer of 2001. I had recently graduated from high school and although I didn't plan on it, I was about to learn that I was a lesbian. Just after graduating, I talked my parents in to allowing me to move into the basement so that I could have more independence while I tried to figure out where I was going in my life.

I had arranged to have a "girl's night in," an idea I'd stolen from a magazine where the females all get together to gossip and gush and leave their male counterparts to their own devices. I'd only invited one friend over since the other girls in my circle had already made other plans, but we planned to make the most of the evening. Andrea promised to be at my house by seven, so I rushed to get everything ready. I had the foresight to have my older sister buy some cheap wine, and I'd prepared some snacks for us.

Andrea was a new friend I met in my belly dancing class about six weeks prior and I was excited to have the chance to get to know her better. She had chosen me as her shoulder to cry on when her boyfriend dumped her for a trashy stripper the week before, so I was already

116

beginning to feel close to her. Andrea was the type of girl I always envied in high school. She was brunette with huge green eyes and full pouty lips. She was tall with long legs, a small waist and amazing curves. She had the kind of tits the guys couldn't keep their eyes off of and wore the tight little tank tops to show them off. Her sexy curves looked even more incredible in her belly dancing costume. The purple mesh bra showed off her gorgeous cleavage while the belt of the skirt sat gently on those banging hips, accentuating an ass that takes all your willpower not to slap.

I had asked Andrea to bring over her dancing costume so we could run through our latest routine and practice a bit. I needed someone to critique my spins and her spins were always on point. I was considering how mouth wateringly sexy she looked in her outfit when a knock at my door startled me out of my daydream. I rushed to answer the door and had to pause before I opened it so that I wouldn't seem too eager. I eased open the door and there stood Andrea, hair in loose curls around her shoulders, ripped jeans showing off her tan legs, and a tight band tee shirt that made me want to throw her down before she could even walk through the door.

I cleared my throat in hopes of clearing my mind. "Hey," I managed.

"Hey, Amy. Sorry if I'm a few minutes early. I thought traffic would be a bit worse than it was. Guess I just got lucky," she said with a flip of her hair as she sauntered through the door.

I helped her with her bag and offered her a glass of wine, apologizing for already having started my own before she'd arrived. Andrea started up some small talk as I carefully poured her a drink. We sat on my hand-me-down couch and talked about anything we could think of for a while until the awkward silences started to become more frequent.

Finally, I asked her if we could work on our dance routines. She agreed and we began to get into our costumes.

I was standing in my new black lace thong, my back to Andrea when I heard her cry out from frustration. "I can never get this stupid thing on right," she whined as she tried to straighten the straps on her top.

"I can help," I offered, forgetting that I was mostly naked.

"That would be awesome. I'm sorry if seeing me undressed makes you uncomfortable. I guess we're both females. It's nothing either one of us hasn't seen before," she said with a light blush that was so adorable it made me jealous of her beauty at the same time it made my pussy wet. I managed a light chuckle and told her that I didn't mind, hoping my eagerness didn't show.

I came up behind her and wrapped my arms around to the front of her, offering to show her the way I put my top on so that I don't get the straps so tangled. As I was untangling her straps, the inside of my wrist grazed her hard nipple. At that same moment, I noticed she had pulled her hair to one side so that it wouldn't be in my way, exposing her soft neck. I lost control.

My mouth gently grazed her shoulder as I kissed her warm skin, taking in her clean, floral scent. She pulled away from me and turned to face me, dropping her hands, her top falling to the floor.

"I'm really sorry. I don't know what just..." I trailed off as she moved in to press her perfect lips against mine. Her mouth was hot and eager. Her hands tangled themselves into my hair while my hands explored her sensuous curves. She let her mouth trail down my chest and began to suck on my nipple. I heard a moan escape my mouth as I felt my panties grow even wetter. I let her play with my tits for a moment before I pushed her down on my bed and pulled her red silk panties down. I could smell her pussy, her heat, her need.

I took her mound into my mouth without hesitation, gently licking her clit as she moaned. My left hand slid down between my own legs as my right hand spread her pussy lips. I sank a finger inside her hot, wet pussy, surprised at the warmth and tightness. Her hands gripped my head and held onto my hair. She pressed my face even deeper into her cunt as I struggled to breathe and continue to make her squirm beneath me. By now she was moaning loudly, fucking my face and suddenly, I had an idea.

Pushing away from her cunt, I told her that this was my first time with a female. She hesitated, looking a bit disappointed. "Don't worry," I hurried to explain. "I'm loving every fucking second of it. It's just that... well... I want you to ride my face," I said with a tiny bit of embarrassment. She jumped up excitedly and pushed me down onto my back. As she started to mount my face, I realized that she was also angling her body so that she could eat my pussy at the same time. Soon, my face was buried deep in her sweet cunt as I could feel her easing her way down to mine. First, I felt her hair tickle my thighs. Then her voluptuous tits grazed my tummy. Next came her warm breath on my bare pussy.

The ecstasy that came next was indescribable. This could not be the first pussy Andrea had eaten! She was amazing. She rode my face, bucking and moaning into my pussy while she licked my clit, fingering my hole and playing with my g-spot. I could feel myself getting closer and closer. I grabbed an ass cheek with one hand while I fingered her snatch with the other. I felt her body tense up as she showered my face with her cum.

Pussy juice dripping down my chin, rolling down my neck, this gorgeous woman trembling with orgasm, fucking my face... I was about to explode. I moaned loudly and began to squirt all over her hand. She quickly realized what was happening as she lowered her face to get a mouthful of my cum.

We collapsed, tangled in each other's bodies. Andrea looked at me and a breathless little giggle escaped her wet lips. She kissed me, mixing her cum with mine, tasting both our pussies in one wet kiss. "I think we're going to have a fantastic friendship, Amy," Andrea said with a huge grin. I had to agree. We spent the rest of the night and the next day in each other's arms. It was then that I realized just what I had been missing while I was dating all those assholes... pussy. Now I can't get enough of it!